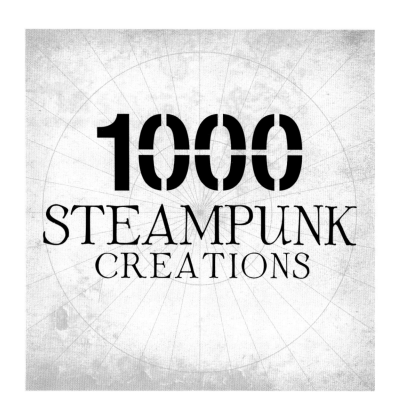

1000
STEAMPUNK
CREATIONS

First published in the United States of America by
Quarry Books, a member of
Quayside Publishing Group
100 Cummings Center
Suite 406-L
Beverly, Massachusetts 01915-6101
Telephone: (978) 282-9590
Fax: (978) 283-2742
www.quarrybooks.com
Visit www.Craftside.Typepad.com for a behind-the-scenes peek at our crafty world!

LIBRARY OF CONGRESS CATALOGING-IN-PUBLICATION DATA
IS AVAILABLE

ISBN-13: 978-1-59253-691-7
ISBN-10: 1-59253-691-3

10 9 8 7 6 5 4 3 2 1

Design and Layout: Sandra Salamony
Front cover images (clockwise from top): James Muscarello, Muscarello Design; Daniel Proulx, Catherinette Rings; Jeffrey Richter; Dr. Grymm Laboratories; Topsy Turvy Design; Jud Turner, Jud Turner, Sculptor, LLC; Christina "Riv" Hawkes; and Dr. Grymm Laboratories
Back cover images (right to left): Eric Freitas; Arthur W. Donovan, Donovan Design; Kyle Cassidy; and Anthony Jon Hicks

Printed in China

1000
STEAMPUNK
CREATIONS

DR. GRYMM

WITH
Barbe Saint John

BEVERLY MASSACHUSETTS

QUARRY BOOKS

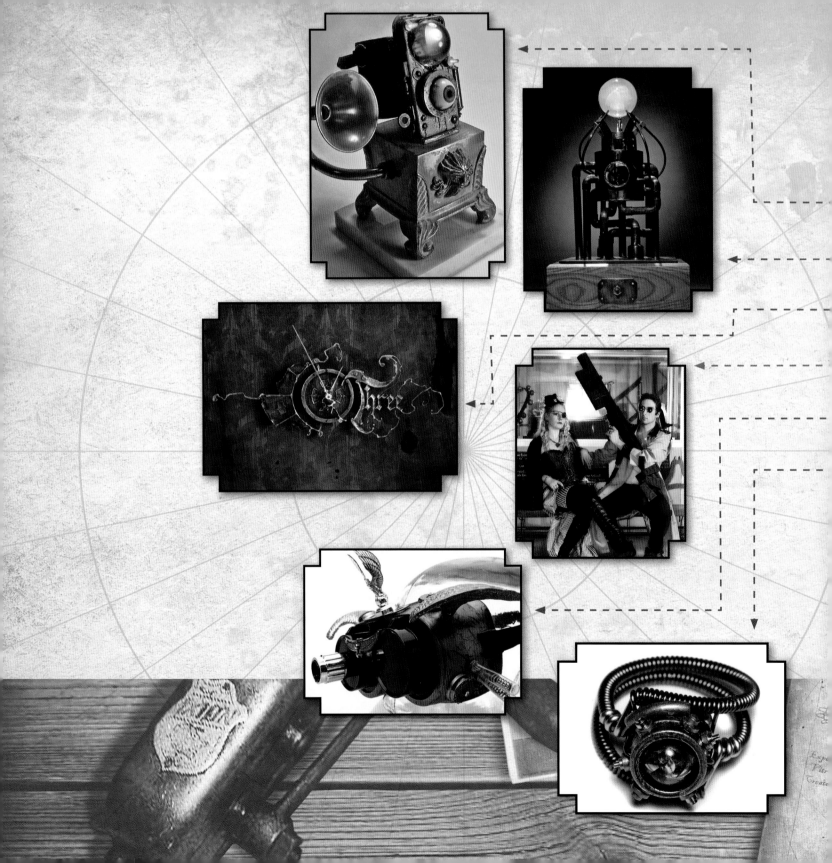

CONTENTS

INTRODUCTION

"Steampunk is the scholar's science fiction." This is the brief description Dr. Grymm Laboratories has come to use to describe the fascinating art movement that seems to have taken the world by storm. Although the descriptive term *Steampunk* was coined in the world of literature within the past thirty years, the origin of the ideas go back much further. Born from the writings of H. G. Welles, Mary Shelley, and Jules Verne and the inventions of Nikola Tesla, Steampunk offers a melding of late 1800s aesthetic with scientific discovery and otherworldly technology. Though Steampunk has reached a tipping point recently, it is not just a current trend. The Steampunk aesthetic has been woven throughout our media and consciousness for more than a century in books, film, music, fashion, and art. Even with a time machine, I'm sure the great-grandparents of science fiction literature would not have imagined that their words and inspirations would have created such a fantastic world.

Today, Steampunk has a fan base that stretches around the globe. Amazing themed events attract well-dressed enthusiasts to maker's fairs, festivals, fashion shows, art exhibits, conventions, musical performances, tea parties, and masquerades. Each enthusiast brings his or her own view of what Steampunk is. The genre appeals to both young and old, and reaches out to inspire even those who would not have considered themselves artists. From the moment fans are compelled to build their first pair of goggles or take apart an old brass lamp from a thrift store and reassemble it into a Victorian weapon, they are hooked. Some choose to recycle from our past to invent beautiful jewelry, contraptions, and props.

Others design and build from scratch, creating epic works of functional art such as clocks, lamps, and vehicles. Still others hone their talents by creating personal character aliases and penning tales about far-off realms where their adventures take place.

Within the pages of this book you will find a collection like no other. From novice to professional, the artists we have brought together celebrate an art movement where a reimagined past is recycled into an unbelievable future. Steampunk artists create an alternate world not bound by the modern millennial conventions of physics, science, and convenience technology. Artists reject the sleek and plastic world we have come to rely on. Steampunk is a chance for artists to build with their hands and their imaginations, just as the great innovators of the industrial revolution did.

Steampunk also creates a tightly knit community. Artists help other artists by inspiring, motivating, and challenging each other to create. While looking through submissions for this book, we were amazed by the amount of talent we had to choose from. This collection of 1,000 images represents a wide variety of styles and mediums to best capture Steampunk in all of its many wondrous facets. Steampunk style is as unique as the person who creates it.

On behalf of the crew at Dr. Grymm Laboratories, I hope you enjoy the fantastic journey these images will take you on. May they inspire you to follow the curious tinkerer who lives inside all of us.

—Dr. Grymm

CHAPTER 1:

MODIFIED
TECHNOLOGY

0001 – 0042 •------▶

0001 **Dr. Grymm**, Dr. Grymm Laboratories, USA

0002 **Derrick Culligan**, USA

• - - - - - ►

0003 **Derrick Culligan**, USA

0004 **Derrick Culligan**, USA

• - - - - - ►

0005 **Derrick Culligan**, USA

- ► *0006* **Dr. Grymm**, Dr. Grymm Laboratories, USA

0007 **Derrick Culligan**, USA

0008 **Jordan Waraksa**, USA

0009 **The Lord Baron Joseph C.R. Vourteque IV & Rev. Cpt. Samuel Flint**, USA

●- ► *0010* **The Lord Baron Joseph C.R. Vourteque IV & Rev. Cpt. Samuel Flint**, USA

0011 **The Lord Baron Joseph C.R. Vourteque IV & Rev. Cpt. Samuel Flint**, USA

0012 **The Lord Baron Joseph C.R. Vourteque IV** & **Rev. Cpt. Samuel Flint**, USA

0013   **Michael Salerno**, USA

0014 **Professor Thaddeus T. Fang a.k.a. artist Anthony J. Rogers III**, USA

•---► 0015 **Professor Thaddeus T. Fang a.k.a. artist Anthony J. Rogers III**, USA

0016 **Urbandon**, Australia

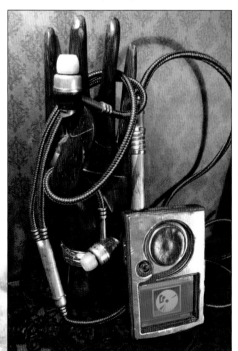

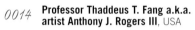

0017 **Sara Gries**, USA

•------► 0018 **Sara Gries**, USA

0019 **Will Rockwell**, USA

0020 **Michael Salerno**, USA

0021 **Robert LaMonte**, USA

0022 **Urbandon**, Australia

0023 **Weirdward Works / Arpad Tota**, Hungary

0024 **Weirdward Works / Arpad Tota**, Hungary

0025 **Urbandon**, Australia

0026 **Urbandon**, Australia

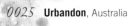

0027 **Weirdward Works / Arpad Tota**, Hungary ● - - - - - - - - ► *0028* **Weirdward Works / Arpad Tota**, Hungary

0029 **Will Rockwell**, USA

0030 **Weirdward Works / Arpad Tota**, Hungary ● - - - - - - - - ► *0031* **Weirdward Works / Arpad Tota**, Hungary

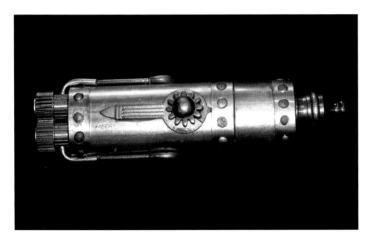

0032 **Will Rockwell**, USA

0033 **Donna Kishbaugh**, The Art of Donna, USA

0034 **Azirca**, New Zealand

0035 **Azirca**, New Zealand

0036 **Roger Wood**, klockwerks, Canada

0037 **Paul Davidson**, USA

0038 **Sara Gries**, USA

● - - - - - - - - - - - - - ▶ 0039 **Sara Gries**, USA

0040 **Paul Davidson**, USA

0041 **Paul Davidson**, USA

0042 **Paul Davidson**, USA

Chapter II:

FINE ART AND SCULPTURE

0043 – 0338 •-----➤

0043 **Jeffrey Richter**, USA

0044 **Jeffrey Richter**, USA

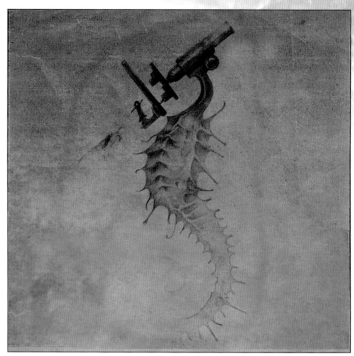

0045 **Jeffrey Richter**, USA

0046 **Jeffrey Richter**, USA

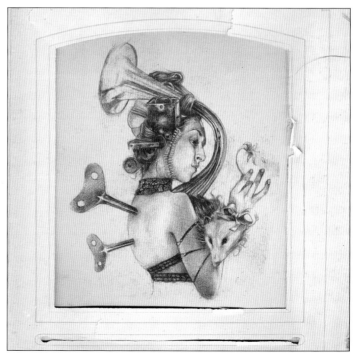

0047 **Jeffrey Richter**, USA

25

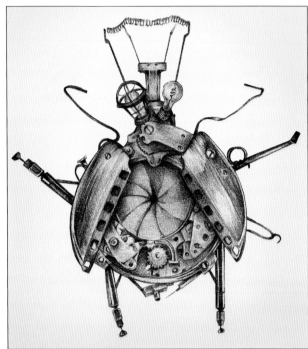

0048 **Jeffrey Richter**, USA

0049 **Jeffrey Richter**, USA

0050 **Jeffrey Richter**, USA

0051 **Martin Horspool**, Australia

0052   **Elizabeth Marek**, Artisan Cake Company, USA

0054 **Jasmine Becket-Griffith**, USA

0053 **Jasmine Becket-Griffith**, USA

0055 **Jasmine Becket-Griffith**, USA

0056 **Christi Friesen**, CF Originals, USA

0057 **Christi Friesen**, CF Originals, USA

0058 **Jason Brammer**, USA

0059 **Jason Brammer**, USA

0060 **Jason Brammer**, USA

0061 **Jud Turner**, Jud Turner, Sculptor, LLC, USA

0062 **Jud Turner**, Jud Turner, Sculptor, LLC, USA

0063 **Jud Turner**, Jud Turner, Sculptor, LLC, USA

0064 **Jud Turner**, Jud Turner, Sculptor, LLC, USA

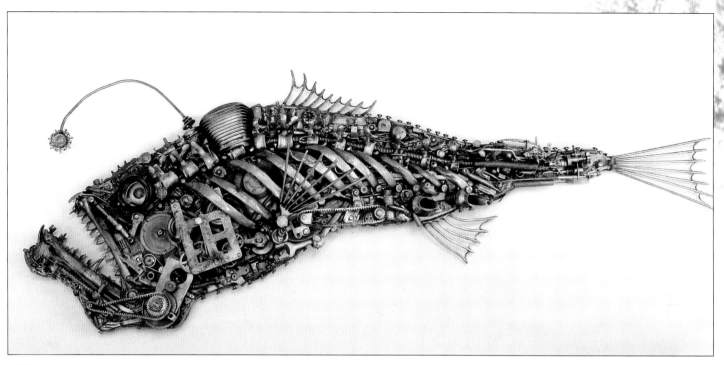

0065 **Jud Turner**, Jud Turner, Sculptor, LLC, USA

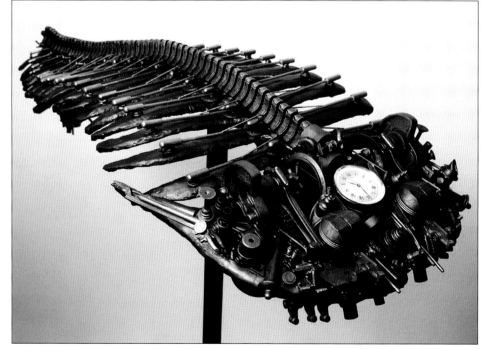

0066 **Jud Turner**, Jud Turner, Sculptor, LLC, USA

0067 **Jud Turner**, Jud Turner, Sculptor, LLC, USA

0068 **Jud Turner**, Jud Turner, Sculptor, LLC, USA

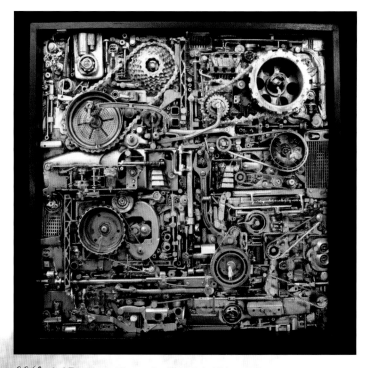

0069 **Jud Turner**, Jud Turner, Sculptor, LLC, USA

●- - - - - - - ▶ *0070* **Jud Turner**, Jud Turner, Sculptor, LLC, USA

0071 **Chadwick**, Australia ● – – – – – ▶ *0072* **Chadwick**, Australia

0073 **Claudia Roulier**, USA

0074 **Jud Turner**, Jud Turner, Sculptor, LLC, USA ● – – – – – – ▶ *0075* **Jud Turner**, Jud Turner, Sculptor, LLC, USA

0076 **Kyle Cassidy**, USA

0077 **Kyle Cassidy**, USA

●--► 0078 **Kyle Cassidy**, USA

0079 **Kyle Cassidy**, USA

0080 **Kyle Cassidy**, USA

0081 **Kyle Cassidy**, USA

0082 **Kyle Cassidy**, USA

0083 **Mel Kolstad**, Snizzers & Gwoo, USA

0084 **Mel Kolstad**, Snizzers & Gwoo, USA

0085 **Mel Kolstad**, Snizzers & Gwoo, USA

0086 **InSectus Artifacts**, Australia

0087 **InSectus Artifacts**, Australia

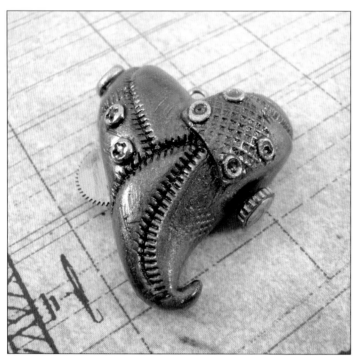

0088 **Kimberly Hart**, Monster Kookies, Canada

0089 **Kimberly Hart**, Monster Kookies, Canada

0090 **Kimberly Hart**, Monster Kookies, Canada

0091 **Kimberly Hart**, Monster Kookies, Canada

0092 **Kimberly Hart**, Monster Kookies, Canada

0093 **Kimberly Hart**, Monster Kookies, Canada

0094 **Kimberly Hart**, Monster Kookies, Canada

0095 **Kimberly Hart**, Monster Kookies, Canada

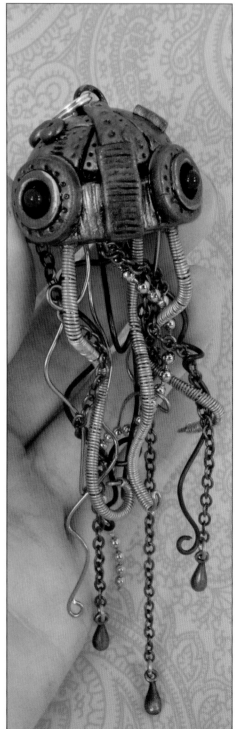

0096 **Kimberly Hart**, Monster Kookies, Canada

0097 **Kimberly Hart**, Monster Kookies, Canada

0098 **Kimberly Hart**, Monster Kookies, Canada

0099 **Kimberly Hart**, Monster Kookies, Canada

0100 **Anthony Jon Hicks**, Tinplate Studios, USA

0101   **Melissa Williams**, USA

0102   **Melissa Williams**, USA

0103   **Melissa Williams**, USA

0104   **Melissa Williams**, USA

0105 **Melissa Williams**, USA

0106 **Melissa Williams**, USA

0107 **Melissa Williams**, USA

0108 **Melissa Williams**, USA

0109 **Melissa Williams**, USA

0110 **Melissa Williams**, USA

0111 **Melissa Williams**, USA

0112 **Melissa Williams**, USA

0113 **Emperor of the Red Fork Empire**, USA

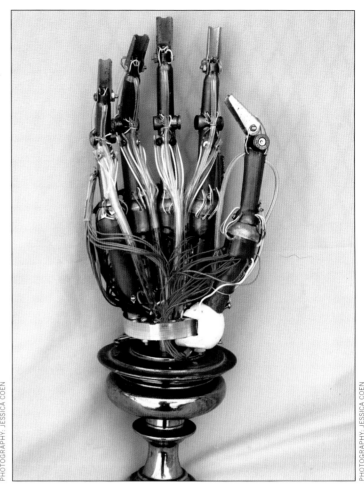

0114 **Emperor of the Red Fork Empire**, USA

0115 **Emperor of the Red Fork Empire**, USA

0116 **Emperor of the Red Fork Empire**, USA

0117 **Royal Steamline**, USA

0118   **Royal Steamline,** USA

0119   **Royal Steamline,** USA

0120   **Royal Steamline,** USA

0121　**Dominique Falla,** Australia

0122　**Dominique Falla,** Australia

0123　**Dominique Falla,** Australia

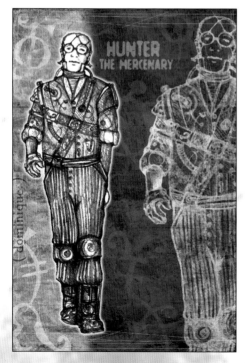

0124　**Dominique Falla,** Australia

0125　**Dominique Falla,** Australia

0126　**Dominique Falla,** Australia

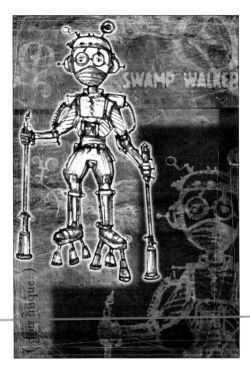

0127 **Dominique Falla,** Australia

0128 **Dominique Falla,** Australia

0129 **Dominique Falla,** Australia

0130 **Dominique Falla,** Australia

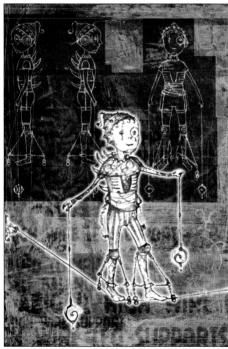

0131 **Dominique Falla,** Australia

0132 **Dominique Falla,** Australia

0133 **Martin Horspool**, Australia

0134 **Martin Horspool**, Australia

0135 **Martin Horspool**, Australia

0136 **Martin Horspool**, Australia

0137　**Martin Horspool**, Australia

0138 **Martin Horspool**, Australia

0139 **Martin Horspool**, Australia

0140 **Martin Horspool**, Australia

0141 **Martin Horspool**, Australia

0142 **Martin Horspool**, Australia

0143 **Martin Horspool**, Australia

0144 **Martin Horspool**, Australia

0145 **Martin Horspool**, Australia

0146 **Martin Horspool**, Australia

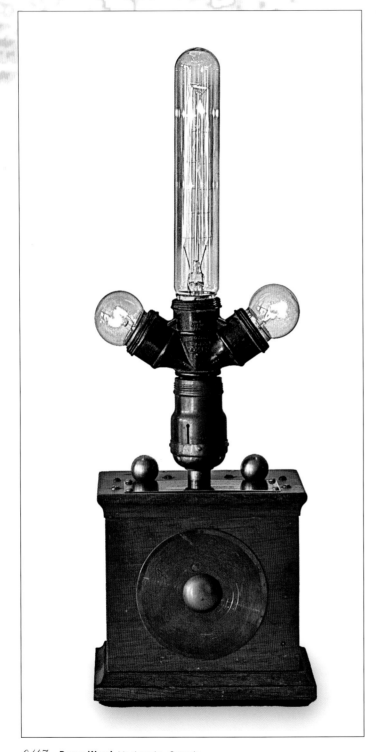

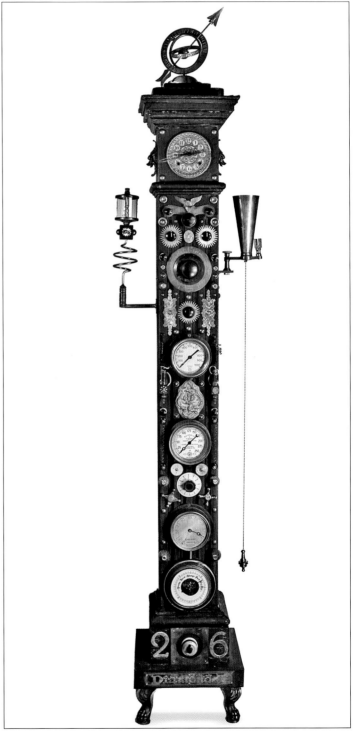

0147 **Roger Wood**, klockwerks, Canada

0148 **Roger Wood**, klockwerks, Canada

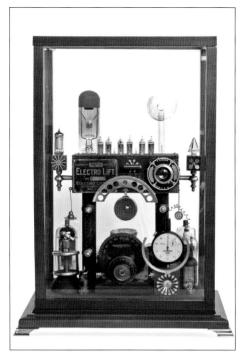

0149 **Roger Wood**, klockwerks, Canada

0150 **Isaiah Max Plovnick**, USA

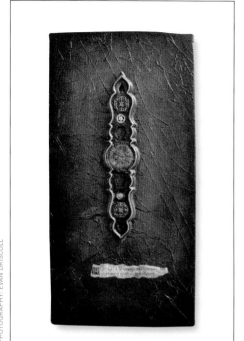

0151 **Jessica M. Coen**, USA

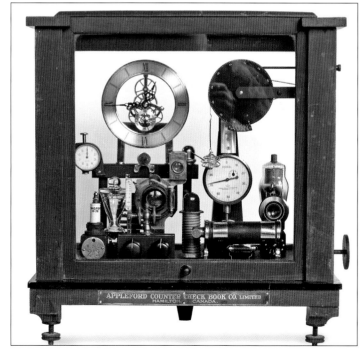

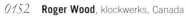

0152 **Roger Wood**, klockwerks, Canada

0153 **Jessica M. Coen**, USA

"A Stitch in Time"

0154 **Dr. Grymm**, Dr. Grymm Laboratories, USA

1902 · Pug denied Martian space travel

0155 **Dr. Grymm**, Dr. Grymm Laboratories, USA

1900 – Pug realizes this is NOT a fire hydrant

0156 **Dr. Grymm**, Dr. Grymm Laboratories, USA

So THIS is where French Poodles come from? MAGNIFIQUE!

0157 **Dr. Grymm**, Dr. Grymm Laboratories, USA

-THE NEW LAB ASSISTANT-
"This is why we cant have nice things"

0158 **Dr. Grymm**, Dr. Grymm Laboratories, USA

Pug was hoping for chamomile tea

0159 **Dr. Grymm**, Dr. Grymm Laboratories, USA

-How the Grymm Stole Christmas-
"Whoville is in trouble this year"

0160 **Dr. Grymm**, Dr. Grymm Laboratories, USA

1884 - Pug concerned about the giant cats

0161 **Dr. Grymm**, Dr. Grymm Laboratories, USA

0162 **Dr. Grymm**, Dr. Grymm Laboratories, USA

PHOTOGRAPHY: TIM MARCHAND, AJAR COMMUNICATIONS

0163 **Daniel Proulx**, Catherinette Rings, Canada

PHOTOGRAPHY: SCHENCK AND SCHENCK PHOTOGRAPHY

164 **Terrill Helander**, Art My Way, USA

0165 **Daniel Proulx**, Catherinette Rings, Canada

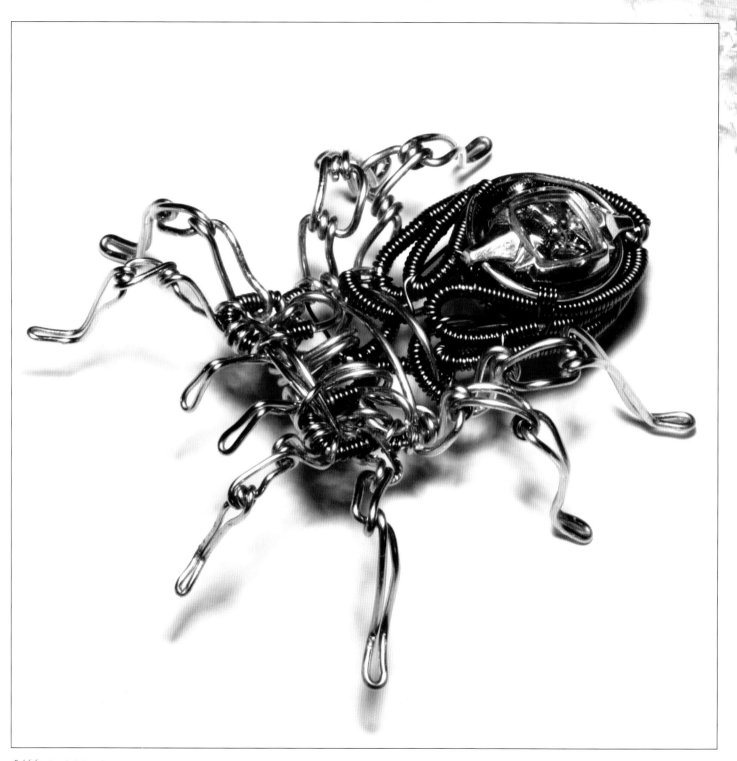

0166 **Daniel Proulx**, Catherinette Rings, Canada

0167 **Christopher Mark Perez**, USA

0168 **Christopher Mark Perez**, USA

0169 **Christopher Mark Perez**, USA

0170 **Christopher Mark Perez**, USA

0171 **Christopher Mark Perez**, USA

0172 **Christopher Mark Perez**, USA

0173   **Christopher Mark Perez**, USA

0174   **Christopher Mark Perez**, USA

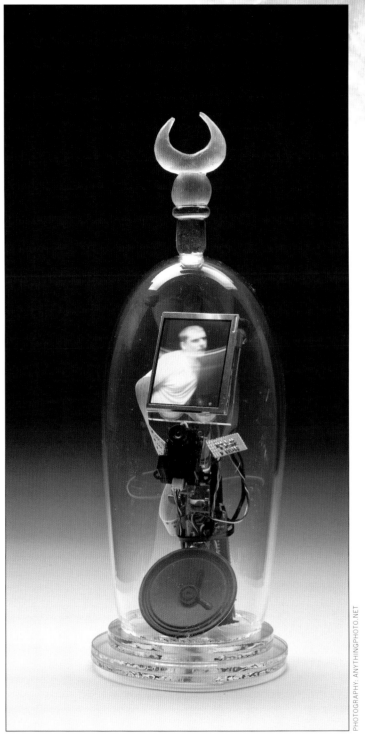

0175   **Tim Tate**, Washington Glass School, USA

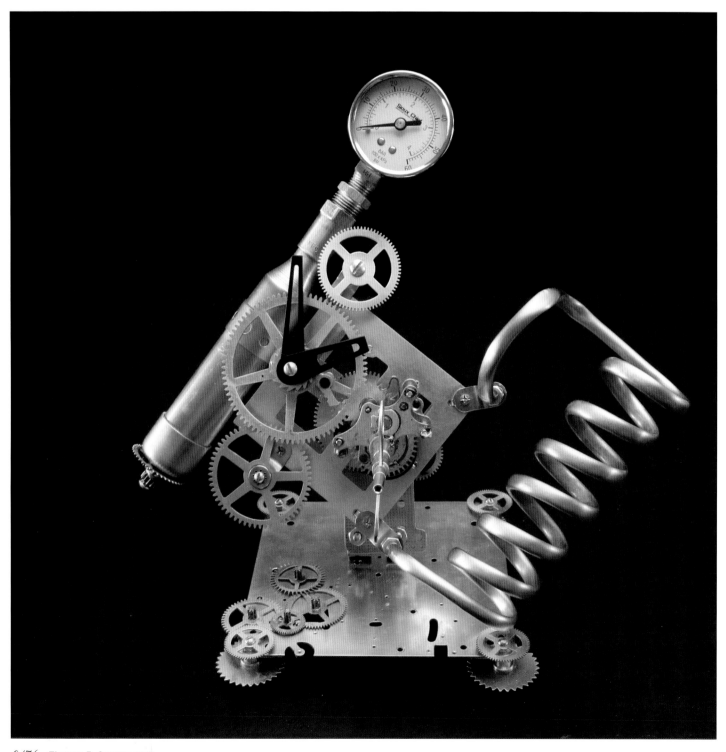

0176 **Thomas E. Gawron**, USA

0177 **Thomas E. Gawron**, USA •----▶ *0178* **Thomas E. Gawron**, USA   *0179* **Jenifer J. Renzel**, USA

0180 **Thomas E. Gawron**, USA •----▶ *0181* **Thomas E. Gawron**, USA   *0182* **Jenifer J. Renzel**, USA

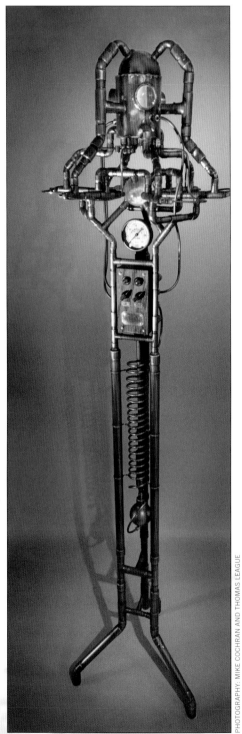

0183 **Mike Cochran**, USA ● - - - - - ▶

0184 **Mike Cochran**, USA ● - - - - - ▶

0185 **Mike Cochran**, USA

0186 **Mike Cochran**, USA

0187 **Mike Cochran**, USA ◀ - - - -

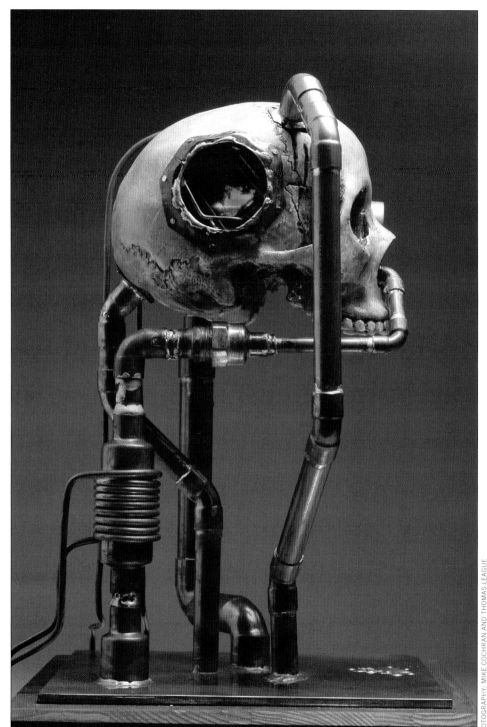

0189　**Michael Pukáč**, USA

0190　**Michael Pukáč**, USA

- • 0188　**Mike Cochran**, USA

PHOTOGRAPHY: MIKE COCHRAN AND THOMAS LEAGUE

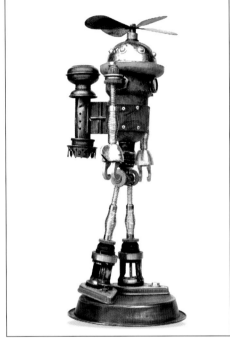

0191 **Dan Jones**, Tinkerbots, USA

0192 **Dan Jones**, Tinkerbots, USA

●--▶ 0193 **Dan Jones**, Tinkerbots, USA

0194 **Dan Jones**, Tinkerbots, USA

0195 **Dan Jones**, Tinkerbots, USA

0196   **Dan Jones**, Tinkerbots, USA

0197   **Dan Jones**, Tinkerbots, USA

0198   **Dan Jones**, Tinkerbots, USA

0199 **Michael Pukáč**, USA

0200 **Michael Pukáč**, USA

0201 **Michael Pukáč**, USA

0202 **Michael Pukáč**, USA

0203　**Michael Pukáč**, USA

0204 **Phillip Valdez**, USA

0205 **Phillip Valdez**, USA

0206 **Markus Schuetz**, Germany

0207 **Markus Schuetz**, Germany

0209 **Markus Schuetz**, Germany

0208 **James Matthew Day**, Notebook
Paper Comics Productions, USA

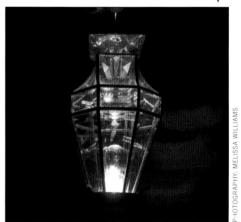

0210 **James Matthew Day**, Notebook
Paper Comics Productions, USA

0211 **Judy A. Anderson,** USA

0212 **Judy A. Anderson**, USA

0213 **Judy A. Anderson**, USA

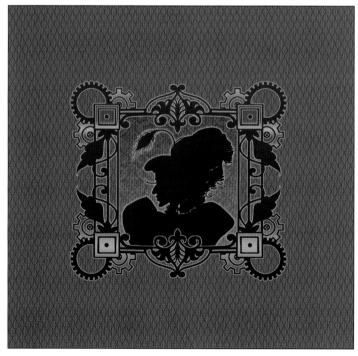

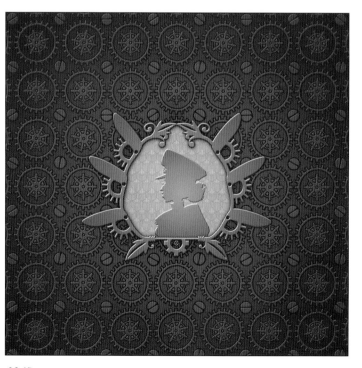

0214 **Jade Gordon**, USA

0215 **Jade Gordon**, USA

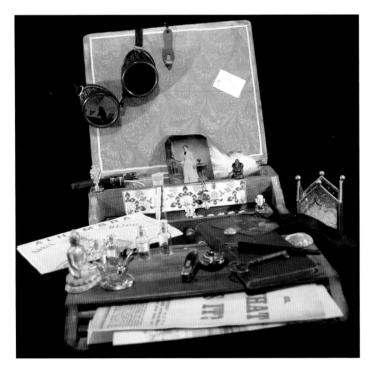

0216 **NG Coonce-Ewing**, Cricket Creations, USA

●- - - - - - - ► 0217 **NG Coonce-Ewing**, Cricket Creations, USA

0218 **NG Coonce-Ewing**, Cricket Creations, USA

0219 **NG Coonce-Ewing**, Cricket Creations, USA

0220 **NG Coonce-Ewing**, Cricket Creations, USA

0221 **NG Coonce-Ewing**, Cricket Creations, USA

0222 **Barbe Saint John**, Saints & Sinners, USA

0223 **Billie Robson**, Art By Canace, USA

0224 **Jade Gordon**, USA

0225 **K.Leistikow**, USA

0226 **Mark E. Adams** and **Journeyman**, USA

0227 **Barbe Saint John**, Saints & Sinners, USA

0228 **NG Coonce-Ewing**, Cricket Creations, USA

0229 **Regina Portscheller**, Omnium-Gatherum Arts, USA

0230 **Deanne Smith**, Goldenthrush, USA

0231 **Dr. Grymm** with **James Marsocci**, USA

0232 **Ned Hobgood**, USA

0233 **Billie Robson**, Art By Canace, USA

0234 **Will Rockwell**, USA

There are certain moments, particularly in childhood, when space, time, and even the walls between worlds become Transparent.

Skeptics say it must be some trick of the light. But Courage and a True Heart, each kept like a treasure, will give us a safe passage through.

0235 **Sarah Fishburn**, Designs & Ragtags, USA

0236 **Louise Kiner**, Canada

0237 **Louise Kiner**, Canada

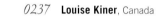

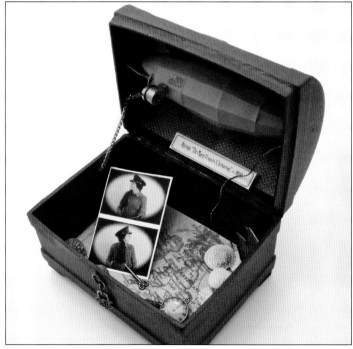

0238 **Louise Kiner**, Canada

0239 **Louise Kiner**, Canada

0240 **Melissa Capyk**, Wild Cakes, Canada
Topper: Builders Studio

0241 **Sandi Billingsley**, USA

Adam the Mechanical Marvel
Manchester - 1867

0242 **Peter Hollinghurst**, UK

0243 **Azirca**, New Zealand ●----▾

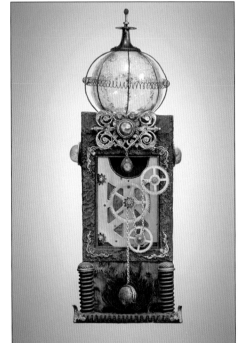

0244 **Azirca**, New Zealand ●----▾

0245 **Azirca**, New Zealand ●----▾

0246 **Azirca**, New Zealand

0247 **Azirca**, New Zealand

0248 **Azirca**, New Zealand

0249 **Azirca**, New Zealand

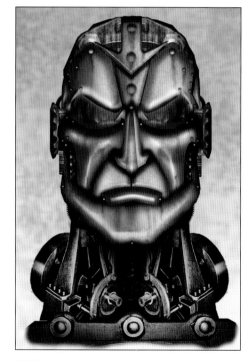

0250 **Dr. Grymm** with **James Muscarello**, USA

0251 **Danny Warner**, USA

0252 **Dr. Grymm** with **James Muscarello**, USA

0253 **Dr. Grymm** with **James Muscarello**, USA

0254 **Dr. Grymm**, Dr. Grymm Laboratories, USA

0255 **Lotus L. Vele**, USA ●‑ ‑ ‑ ‑ ‑ ➤ 0256 **Lotus L. Vele**, USA ●‑ ‑ ‑ ‑ ‑ ➤ 0257 **Lotus L. Vele**, USA

0258 **Lindsey Goodbun**, UK

0259 **Michael J. Marchand** and **Tim Marchand**, Ajar Communications, LLC, USA

0260 **Michael J. Marchand** and **Tim Marchand**, Ajar Communications, LLC, USA

0261 **Michael J. Marchand** and **Tim Marchand**, Ajar Communications, LLC, USA

0262 **Michael J. Marchand** and **Tim Marchand**, Ajar Communications, LLC, USA

0263 **Michael J. Marchand** and **Tim Marchand**, Ajar Communications, LLC, USA

0264 **Michael J. Marchand** and **Tim Marchand**, Ajar Communications, LLC, USA

0265 **Michael J. Marchand** and **Tim Marchand**, Ajar Communications, LLC, USA

0266 **Michael J. Marchand** and **Tim Marchand**, Ajar Communications, LLC, USA

0267 **Michael J. Marchand** and **Tim Marchand**, Ajar Communications, LLC, USA

0268 **Michael J. Marchand** and **Tim Marchand**, Ajar Communications, LLC, USA

0269 **Michael J. Marchand** and **Tim Marchand**, Ajar Communications, LLC, USA

0270 **Michael J. Marchand** and **Tim Marchand**, Ajar Communications, LLC, USA

0271 **Michael J. Marchand** and **Tim Marchand**, Ajar Communications, LLC, USA

0272 **Michael J. Marchand** and **Tim Marchand**, Ajar Communications, LLC, USA

PHOTOGRAPHY: JESSICA COEN

0273 **Emperor of the Red Fork Empire**, USA

PHOTOGRAPHY: JESSICA COEN

0274 **Emperor of the Red Fork Empire**, USA

PHOTOGRAPHY: JESSICA COEN

0275 **Emperor of the Red Fork Empire**, USA

PHOTOGRAPHY: JESSICA COEN

0276 **Emperor of the Red Fork Empire**, USA

PHOTOGRAPHY: JESSICA COEN

● - - - - - - - ▶ *0277* **Emperor of the Red Fork Empire**, USA

0279 **Diana Vick**, USA

0278 **Emperor of the Red Fork Empire**, USA

0280 **Diana Vick**, USA

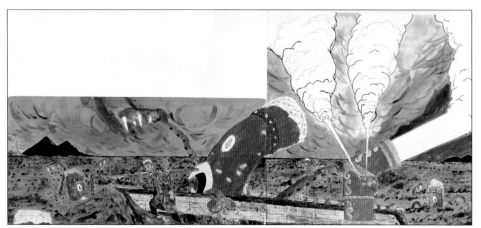

0281 **James Matthew Day**, Notebook Paper Comics Productions, USA

0282 **Diana Laurence**, USA

0283 **K.Leistikow**, USA

0284 **K.Leistikow**, USA

0285 **Diana Laurence**, USA

0286 **Joanne Archer**, The Crow Road, UK

0287 **James Muscarello**, USA

0288 **James Muscarello**, USA

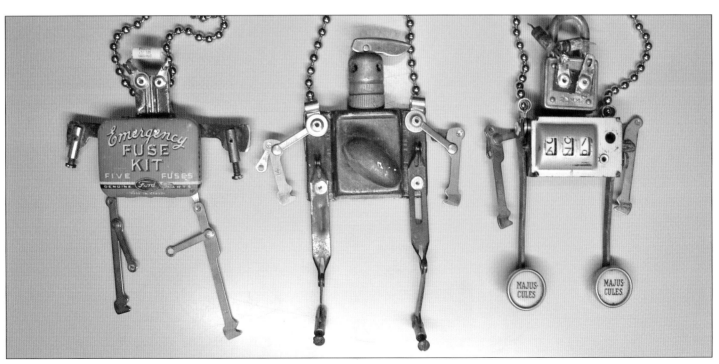

0289 **Martin Horspool**, Australia

0291 **Captain Jason Redbeard**–Royal
Gronican Navy, USA

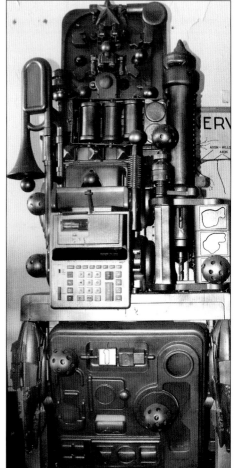

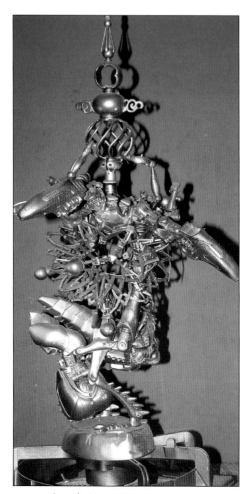

0292 **Captain Jason Redbeard**–Royal
Gronican Navy, USA

0290 **Captain Jason Redbeard**–Royal
Gronican Navy, USA

0293 **Captain Jason Redbeard**–Royal
Gronican Navy, USA

0294 **Captain Jason Redbeard**–Royal
Gronican Navy, USA

0295 **Captain Jason Redbeard**–Royal
Gronican Navy, USA

0296 **Captain Jason Redbeard**–Royal
Gronican Navy, USA

0297 **Captain Jason Redbeard**–Royal
Gronican Navy, USA

0298 **Captain Jason Redbeard**–Royal
Gronican Navy, USA

0299 **Captain Jason Redbeard**–Royal
Gronican Navy, USA

0300   **Captain Jason Redbeard**–Royal Gronican Navy, USA

0301   **Captain Jason Redbeard**–Royal Gronican Navy, USA

0302   **Captain Jason Redbeard**–Royal Gronican Navy, USA

0303   **Captain Jason Redbeard**–Royal Gronican Navy, USA

0304 **Captain Jason Redbeard**–Royal Gronican Navy, USA

0305 **Captain Jason Redbeard**–Royal Gronican Navy, USA

0306 **Captain Jason Redbeard**–Royal Gronican Navy, USA

0307 **Captain Jason Redbeard**–Royal Gronican Navy, USA

0308 **Joshua A. Dinunzio**,
Salty Slug Industries, USA

•----► 0309 **Joshua A. Dinunzio**,
Salty Slug Industries, USA

•---► 0310 **Joshua A. Dinunzio**,
Salty Slug Industries, USA

0311   **Matthew Borgatti**, Sleek and Destroy, USA

0312   **Jeffrey W. Lilley**, USA

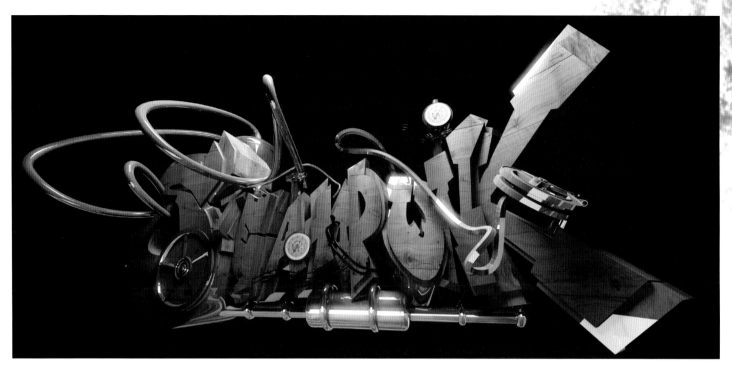

0313   **Graffiti Technica**, Australia

0314   **Martin Horspool**, Australia

0315　**Sheri Jurnecka**, Jurnecka Creations, USA

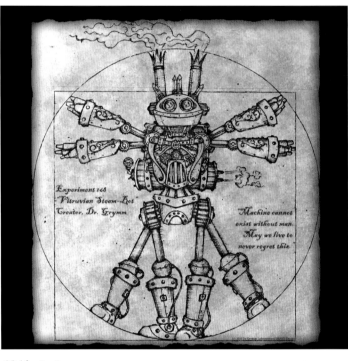

0316　**Dr. Grymm**, Dr. Grymm Laboratories, USA

0317　**Sheri Jurnecka**, Jurnecka Creations, USA

● — — — — — — — ► 0318　**Sheri Jurnecka**, Jurnecka Creations, USA

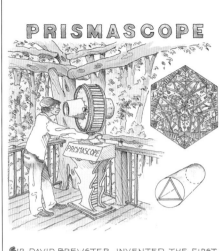

PRISMASCOPE

SIR DAVID BREWSTER INVENTED THE FIRST KALEIDOSCOPE IN 1816. PRODUCING A *PHENOMENON* OF LIGHT & COLOR, THE OPTICAL DEVICE WAS CONSIDERED A *PHILOSOPHICAL* INSTRUMENT. THE PRISMASCOPE, SET IN THE LOOKOUT LOFT, IS A GIANT KALEIDOSCOPE THAT CAPTURES & RECREATES THE FOREST'S *MAGICAL* PATTERNS FOR THE 21ST CENTURY DREAMER.

0319   **Rusty Lamer**, Scenic Designer; **Chip Sullivan**, Optic Provocateur, USA

●- - -► 0320   **Rusty Lamer**, Scenic Designer; **Chip Sullivan**, Optic Provocateur, USA

SPECTRASCOPE

Claude lenses

operating mechanism

CLAUDE LORRAIN (1600-1682) CREATED *ROMANTIC & SUBLIME* VIEWS IN HIS LANDSCAPE PAINTINGS. "CLAUDE LENSES" BECAME POPULAR IN THE 18TH CENTURY WITH TOURISTS WHO WANTED TO EXPERIENCE THE SAME *PICTURESQUE EFFECTS.* THE SPECTRASCOPE IS A 21ST CENTURY ADAPTATION OF THE CLAUDE LENS. LOCATED IN THE CANOPY CATHEDRAL, THE SPECTRASCOPE BATHES THE LAKE, LAWN & HILLSIDE IN A NEARLY *INFINITE* VARIETY OF COLORS.

0321   **Rusty Lamer**, Scenic Designer; **Chip Sullivan**, Optic Provocateur, USA

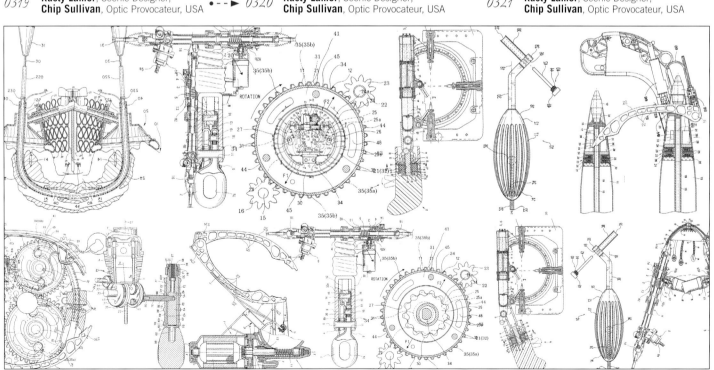

0322   **Danny Warner**, USA

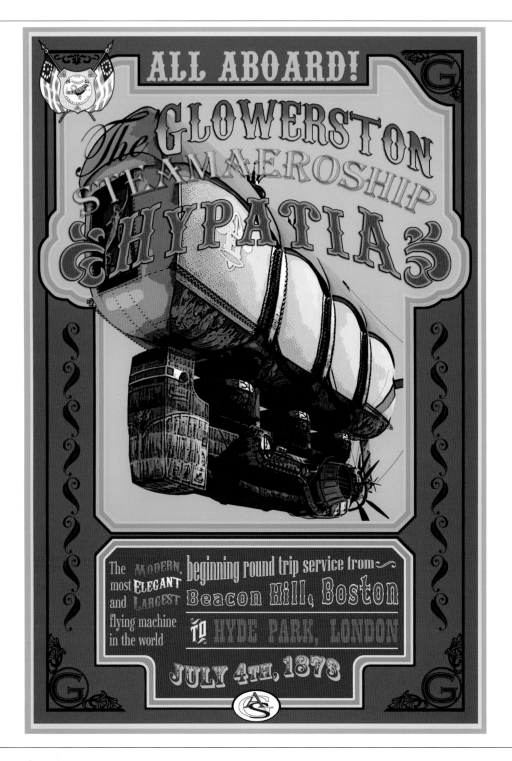

0324 **Eddie Wilson**, whisperstudio broken toys, USA

0325 **Eddie Wilson**, whisperstudio broken toys, USA

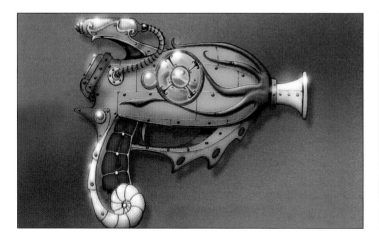

0326 **Dr. Grymm**, Dr. Grymm Laboratories, USA

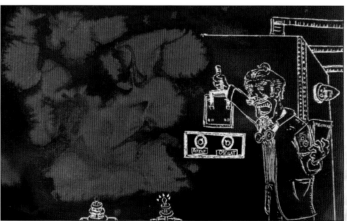

0327 **James Matthew Day**, Notebook Paper Comics Productions, USA

0328 **Tim Tate**,
Washington Glass School, USA

• - - - - ▶ *0329* **Tim Tate**, Washington Glass School, USA

0330 **Eddie Wilson**, whisperstudio
broken toys, USA

0331 **Danny Warner**, USA

0332 **Joshua W. Kinsey**,
J.W. Kinsey's Artifice, USA

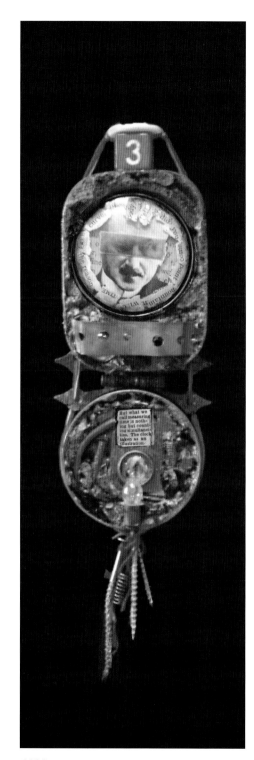

0333 **Laurie Dorrell**, Moonwild Art, USA

0334 **Eddie Wilson**, whisperstudio broken toys, USA

0335 **James Matthew Day**, Notebook Paper Comics Productions, with **Melissa Wiliams**, USA

0336 **Joshua W. Kinsey**, J.W. Kinsey's Artifice, USA

0337 **Martin Horspool**, Australia

0338 **Phillip Valdez**, USA

Chapter III:

HOME DÉCOR

0339 – 0514 •-----►

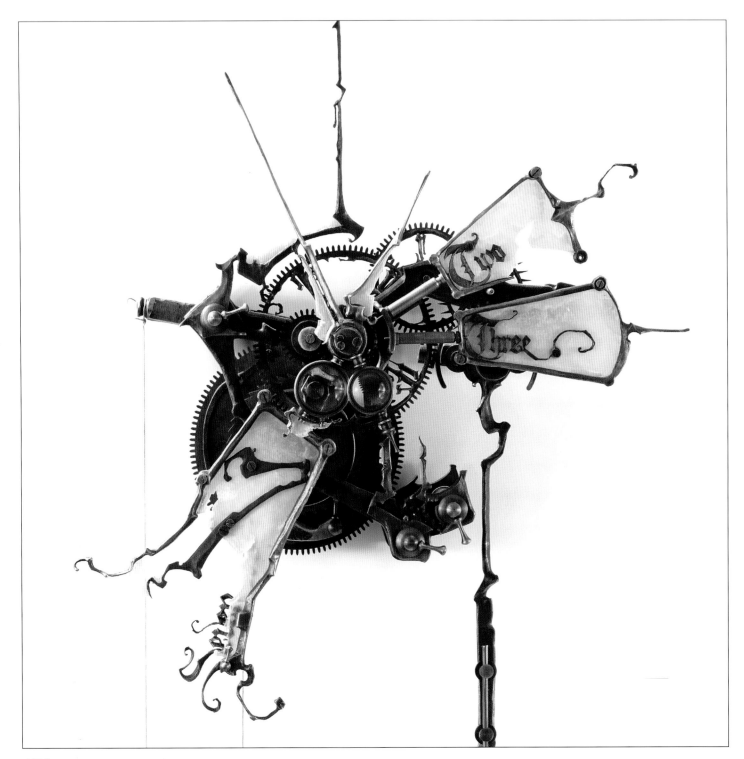

0339 **Eric Freitas**, USA

0340 **Tanya Clarke**, Liquid Light, USA

0341 **Tanya Clarke**, Liquid Light, USA

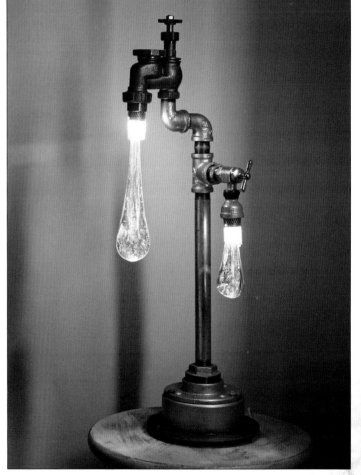

► *0342* **Eric Freitas**, USA

0343 **Tanya Clarke**, Liquid Light, USA

0344 **Eric Freitas**, USA

0345 **Eric Freitas**, USA

0346 **Eric Freitas**, USA

0347 **Eric Freitas**, USA ● - - - - - - - - - - - - - ► 0348 **Eric Freitas**, USA

0349 **Tanya Clarke**, Liquid Light, USA

●-------▶ 0350 **Tanya Clarke**, Liquid Light, USA

0351 **Tanya Clarke**, Liquid Light, USA

0352 **Tanya Clarke**, Liquid Light, USA

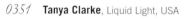 ● - - ► *0353* **Tanya Clarke**, Liquid Light, USA

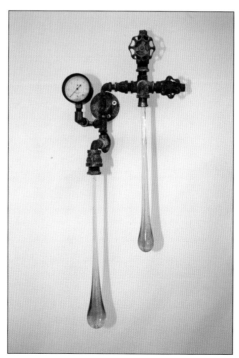

0354 **Tanya Clarke**, Liquid Light, USA

0355 **Tanya Clarke**, Liquid Light, USA

0356 **Tanya Clarke**, Liquid Light, USA

0357 **Tanya Clarke**, Liquid Light, USA ●--►

0358 **Tanya Clarke**, Liquid Light, USA

0359 **Tanya Clarke**, Liquid Light, USA ●--┐

0360 **Tanya Clarke**, Liquid Light, USA ●--►

0361 **Tanya Clarke**, Liquid Light, USA

0362 **Tanya Clarke**, Liquid Light, USA

0363 **Matthew Borgatti**, Sleek and Destroy, USA

0364 **Roger Wood**, klockwerks, Canada

0365 **Roger Wood**, klockwerks, Canada

0366 **Roger Wood**, klockwerks, Canada

0367 **Roger Wood**, klockwerks, Canada

0368 **Roger Wood**, klockwerks, Canada

0369 **Roger Wood**, klockwerks, Canada

0370 **Roger Wood**, klockwerks, Canada

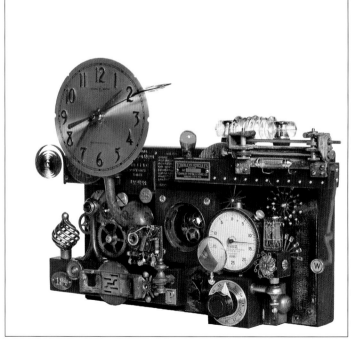

0371 **Roger Wood**, klockwerks, Canada

0372 **Cory Barkman**, Canada

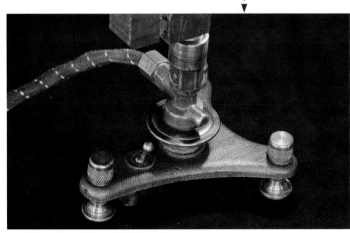

0373 **Cory Barkman**, Canada

0374 **Cory Barkman**, Canada

0375 **Cory Barkman**, Canada

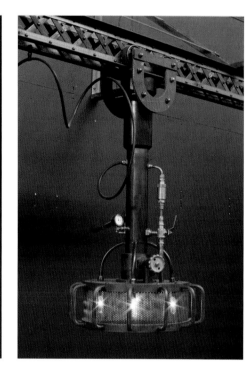

0376 **Cory Barkman**, Canada

0377 **Cory Barkman**, Canada

0378 **Cory Barkman**, Canada

0379 **Cory Barkman**, Canada

0380 **Cory Barkman**, Canada

0381   **LF Roberts**, Floydagain Designs, USA   ● – – – – – – – ►   *0382*   **LF Roberts**, Floydagain Designs, USA

0383   **LF Roberts**, Floydagain Designs, USA   ● – – – – – – – ►   *0384*   **LF Roberts**, Floydagain Designs, USA

HOME DÉCOR

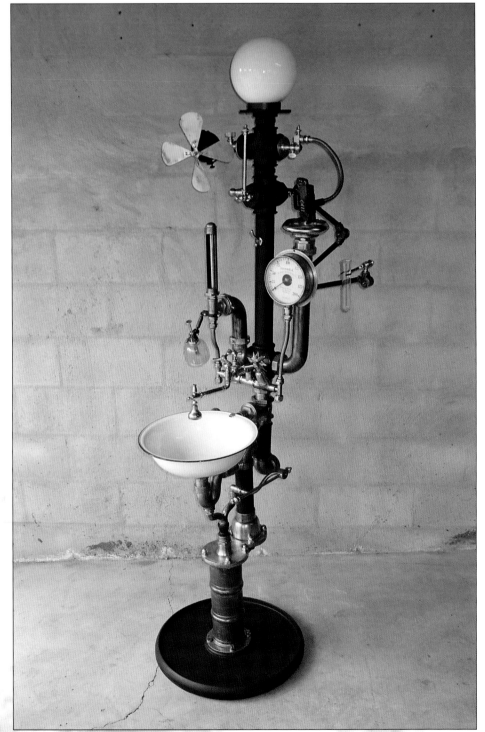

0385 **maduncle**, Australia

0386 **Jordan Waraksa**, USA

0387 **Jordan Waraksa**, USA

0388 **Billie Robson**, Art By Canace, USA

0390 **Billie Robson**, Art By Canace, USA

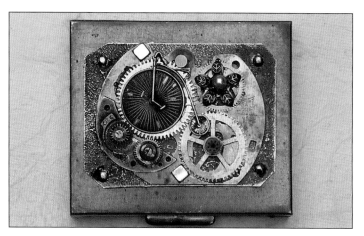

0389 **Billie Robson**, Art By Canace, USA

0391 **Billie Robson**, Art By Canace, USA

0392 **Jeffrey W. Lilley**, USA

0393 **Tanya Clarke**, Liquid Light, USA

0394 **NG Coonce-Ewing**,
Cricket Creations, USA

● - ⌐
▼

0395 **Michael Salerno**, USA

0396 **NG Coonce-Ewing**, Cricket Creations, USA

0398 **Weirdward Works/Arpad Tota**, Hungary

0399 **Weirdward Works/Arpad Tota**, Hungary

0397 **Dr. Grymm**, Dr. Grymm Laboratories, USA

0400 **Weirdward Works/Arpad Tota**, Hungary

0401 **Roger Wood**, klockwerks, Canada

0402 **Roger Wood**, klockwerks, Canada

0403 **Roger Wood**, klockwerks, Canada

0404 **Roger Wood**, klockwerks, Canada

0405 **Roger Wood**, klockwerks, Canada

0406 **Roger Wood**, klockwerks, Canada

0407 **Roger Wood**, klockwerks, Canada

0408 **Roger Wood**, klockwerks, Canada

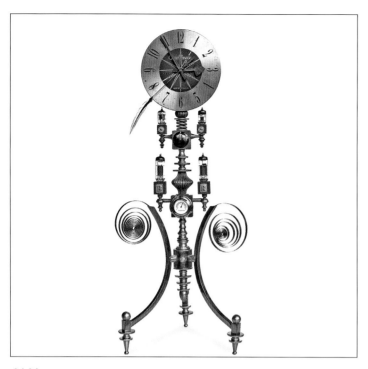

0409 **Roger Wood**, klockwerks, Canada

0410 **Roger Wood**, klockwerks, Canada

0411 **Roger Wood**, klockwerks, Canada

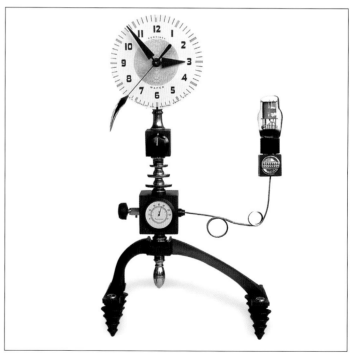

0412 **Roger Wood**, klockwerks, Canada

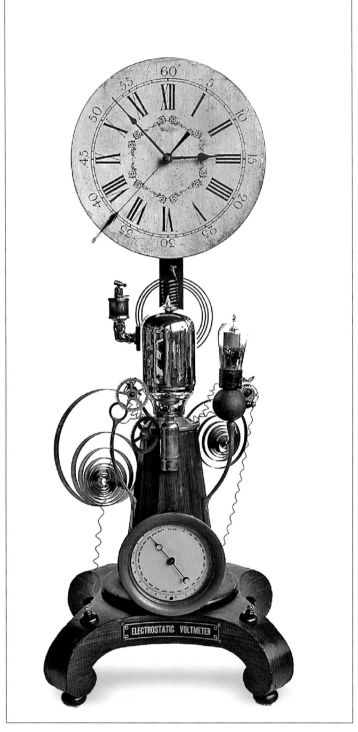

0415 **Christine Cavataio**, USA

0416 **Christine Cavataio**, USA

0417 **Christine Cavataio**, USA

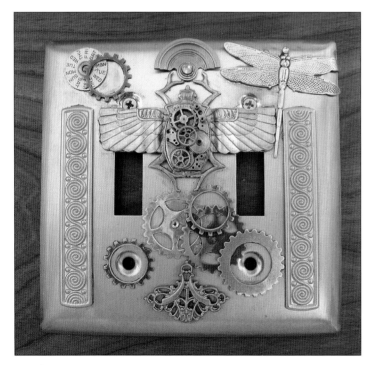

0418 **Christine Cavataio**, USA

0419 **Christine Cavataio**, USA

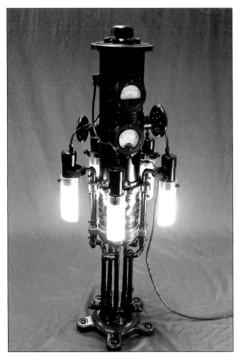

0420 **Joshua W. Kinsey**,
J.W. Kinsey's Artifice, USA

•- - - - - ► 0421 **Joshua W. Kinsey**,
J.W. Kinsey's Artifice, USA

•- - - - - ► 0422 **Joshua W. Kinsey**,
J.W. Kinsey's Artifice, USA

0423 **Joshua W. Kinsey**, J.W. Kinsey's Artifice, USA

•- - - - - - - ► 0424 **Joshua W. Kinsey**, J.W. Kinsey's Artifice, USA

Joshua W. Kinsey,
J.W. Kinsey's Artifice, USA

Joshua W. Kinsey, J.W. Kinsey's Artifice, USA   • - ► *0427* **Joshua W. Kinsey**,
J.W. Kinsey's Artifice, USA

HOME DÉCOR

0428 **Erin Keck**, E.K. Creations, USA

0429 **Will Rockwell**, USA

0430 **Erin Keck**, E.K. Creations, USA

0431 **Erin Keck**, E.K. Creations, USA

0432 **Erin Keck**, E.K. Creations, USA

0433 **Joshua W. Kinsey**, J.W. Kinsey's Artifice, USA

0434 **Erin Keck**, E.K. Creations, USA

0435 **Joshua W. Kinsey**, J.W. Kinsey's Artifice, USA

0436 **Kevin C. Cooper**, Steampunk Kaleidoscopes, UK

•------► 0437 **Kevin C. Cooper**, Steampunk Kaleidoscopes, UK

0438 **Kevin C. Cooper**, Steampunk Kaleidoscopes, UK

•------► 0439 **Kevin C. Cooper**, Steampunk Kaleidoscopes, UK

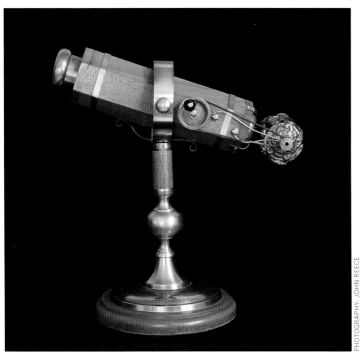

0440 **Kevin C. Cooper**, Steampunk Kaleidoscopes, UK

●------▶ **0441** **Kevin C. Cooper**, Steampunk Kaleidoscopes, UK

0442 **Jessica Faraday**, Faraday Bags and Bijoux, USA

●--------▶ **0443** **Jessica Faraday**, Faraday Bags and Bijoux, USA

0444 **Dillon Works!**, USA

0445 **Dillon Works!**, USA

0446 **Dillon Works!**, USA

0447 **Dillon Works!**, USA

0448 **Lisa A. Rooney**, USA

0449 **Jonathan Gosling**,
River Otter Widget Studios, USA

0450 **Jonathan Gosling**,
River Otter Widget Studios, USA

0451 **Lynne Rutter**, Lynne Rutter
Murals & Decorative Painting, USA

0452 **Lynne Rutter**, Lynne Rutter Murals & Decorative Painting, USA

0453 **Christine Cavataio**, USA

0454 **Christine Cavataio**, USA

0455 **Kammlah.Thayer Collection for Carol Hicks Bolton** / E.J. Victor Furniture, USA

0456　**Joshua W. Kinsey**, J.W. Kinsey's Artifice, USA ● - - - - - - - - ► 0457　**Joshua W. Kinsey**, J.W. Kinsey's Artifice, USA

0458　**Kammlah.Thayer Collection for Carol Hicks Bolton** / E.J. Victor Furniture, USA

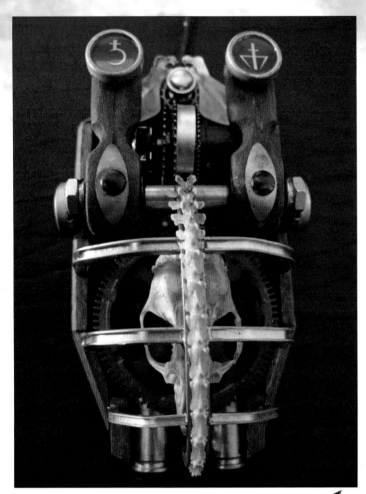

0459 **Daniel Pon**, Paradox Designs, USA

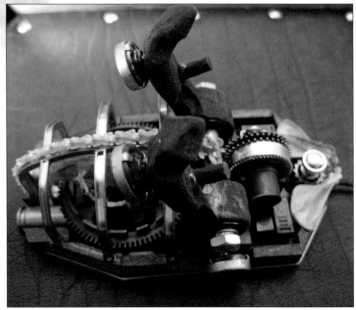

0460 **Daniel Pon**, Paradox Designs, USA

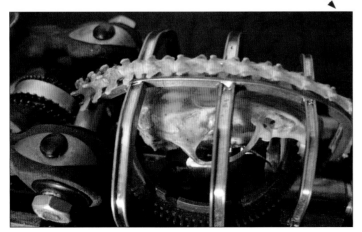

0461 **Daniel Pon**, Paradox Designs, USA

0462 **Daniel Pon**, Paradox Designs, USA

0463 **Heather Simpson-Bluhm**, Bluhm Studios, USA

●--------➤ 0464 **Heather Simpson-Bluhm**, Bluhm Studios, USA

0465 **Tanya Clarke**, Liquid Light, USA

0466 **Will Rockwell**, USA

0467 **Robert Lucas**, Genuine Plastic, USA

0468 **Joshua W. Kinsey**, J.W. Kinsey's Artifice, USA • - - - - - - - - - ▶ 0469 **Joshua W. Kinsey**, J.W. Kinsey's Artifice, USA

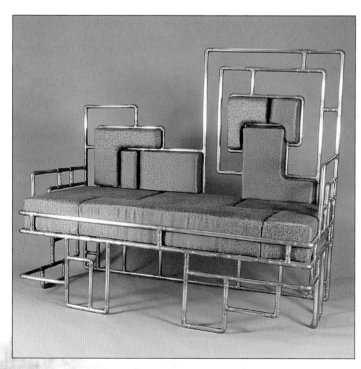

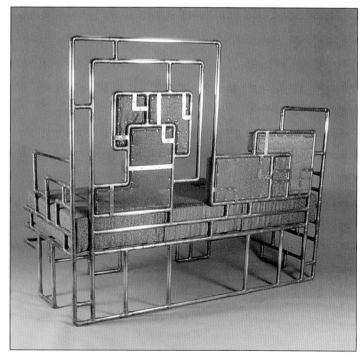

0470 **Tessa J. Chandler**, USA • - - - - - - - - ▶ 0471 **Tessa J. Chandler**, USA

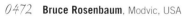

0472　**Bruce Rosenbaum**, Modvic, USA

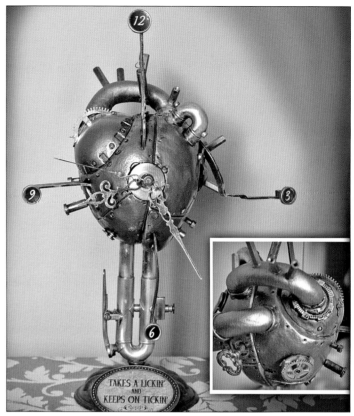

0473　**Dr. Grymm**, Dr. Grymm Laboratories, USA

TAKES A LICKIN'
AND
KEEPS ON TICKIN'

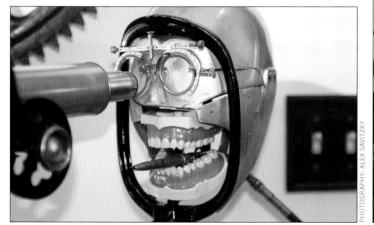

0474　**Bruce Rosenbaum**, Modvic, USA

0475　**Bruce Rosenbaum**, Modvic, USA

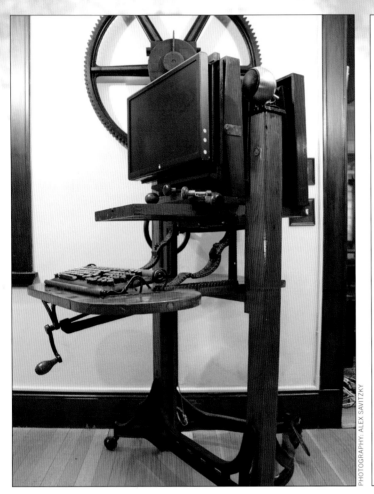

0476 **Bruce Rosenbaum**, Modvic, USA

0477 **Val Lucas**, Bowerbox Press, USA

0478 **Bruce Rosenbaum**, Modvic, USA

0479 **Bruce Rosenbaum**, Modvic, USA

0480 **Cole H. Goldstein**, Cole Hasting's Modern Antiquities, USA

0481 **Cole H. Goldstein**, Cole Hasting's Modern Antiquities, USA

0482 **Cole H. Goldstein**, Cole Hasting's Modern Antiquities, USA

0483 **Lisa A. Rooney**, USA

HOME DÉCOR

0484 **Brace Peters**, USA •------► 0485 **Brace Peters**, USA •------► 0486 **Brace Peters**, USA

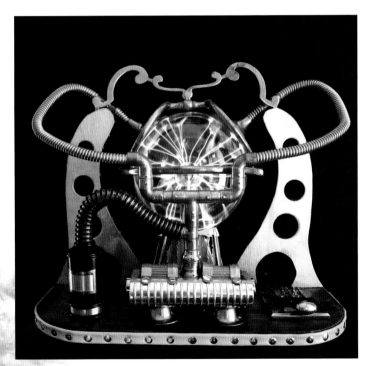

0487 **Will Rockwell**, USA

0488 **Andrew Tarrant**, Trespasser Ceramics, Canada •------

0489 **Bruce Rosenbaum**, Modvic, USA

0490 **Bruce Rosenbaum**, Modvic, USA

● - - - - - - - ▶ 0491 **Bruce Rosenbaum**, Modvic, USA

▶ 0492 **Andrew Tarrant**, Trespasser Ceramics, Canada

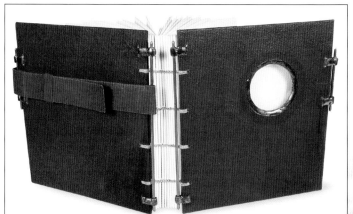

0493 **Val Lucas**, Bowerbox Press, USA

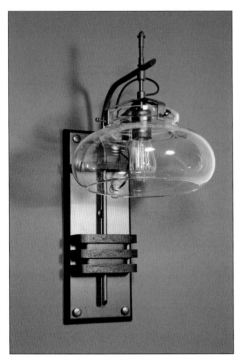

0494 **Arthur W. Donovan**, Donovan Design, USA

0495 **Arthur W. Donovan**, Donovan Design, USA

0496 **Arthur W. Donovan**, Donovan Design, USA

0497 **Arthur W. Donovan**, Donovan Design, USA

0498 **Arthur W. Donovan**, Donovan Design, USA

0500 **Arthur W. Donovan**, Donovan Design, USA

0499 **Arthur W. Donovan**, Donovan Design, USA ●‑‑‑‑‑‑‑‑‑► 0501 **Arthur W. Donovan**, Donovan Design, USA

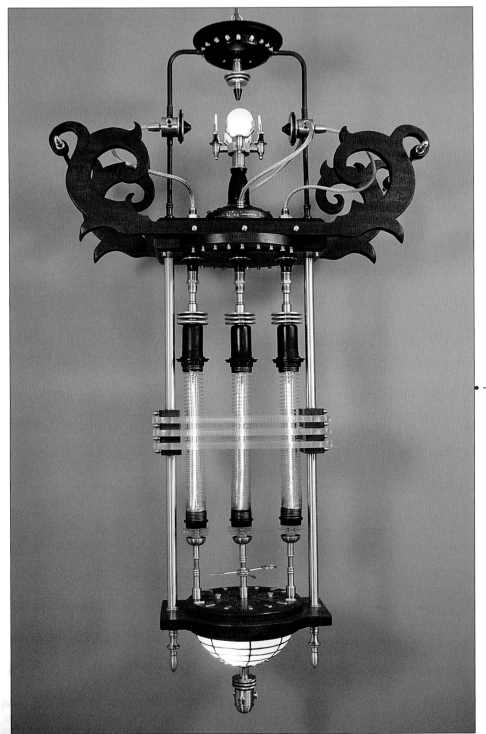

0502 **Arthur W. Donovan**, Donovan Design, USA

0503 **Arthur W. Donovan**, Donovan Design, USA

0504 **Arthur W. Donovan**, Donovan Design, USA

0505 **Arthur W. Donovan**, Donovan Design, USA

0506 **Arthur W. Donovan**, Donovan Design, USA

0507 **Arthur W. Donovan**, Donovan Design, USA

0508 **Arthur W. Donovan**, Donovan Design, USA

0509 **Arthur W. Donovan**, Donovan Design, USA *0510* **Arthur W. Donovan**, Donovan Design, USA *0511* **Arthur W. Donovan**, Donovan Design, USA

0512 **Arthur W. Donovan**, Donovan Design, USA *0513* **Arthur W. Donovan**, Donovan Design, USA

1000 STEAMPUNK CREATIONS

0514 **Arthur W. Donovan**, Donovan Design, USA

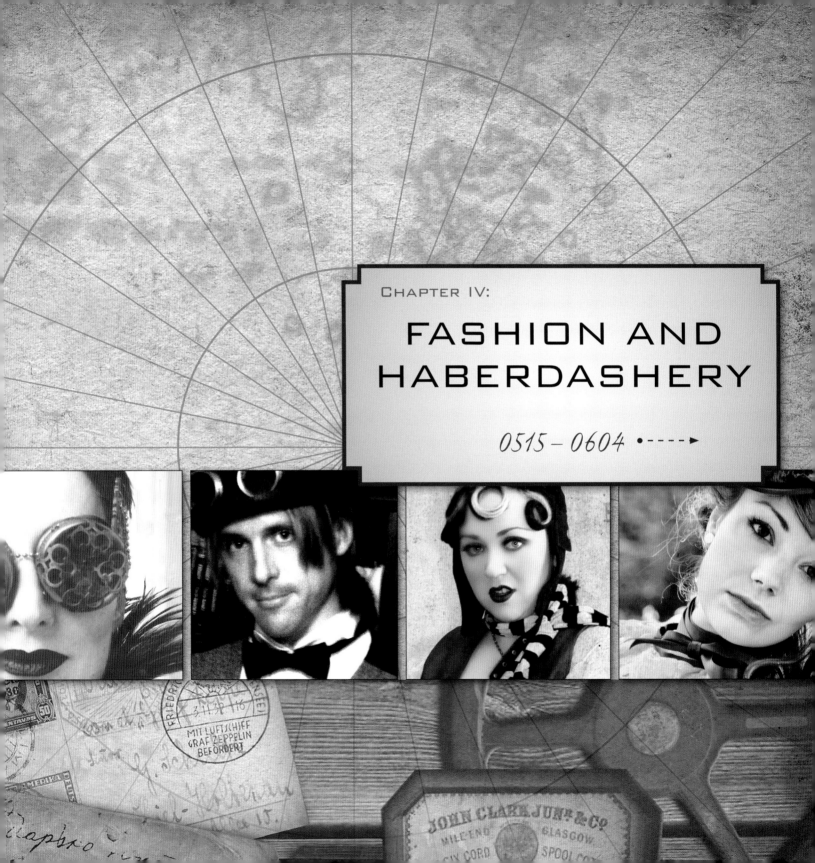

CHAPTER IV:

FASHION AND HABERDASHERY

0515 – 0604 •- - - - ▶

0515   **Topsy Turvy Design**, USA

0516 **P.J. Pilgrim**, Apple Blossom Photography, USA

0517 **Martin Small**, UK

0518 **Martin Small**, UK

0519 **Legion Fantastique**, USA

PHOTOGRAPHY: MARIA S. VARELA, SANTIAGO ALVAREZ

0520 **Penelope Almendros Garcia,**
Revue Vintage, Spain

PHOTOGRAPHY: SILENT SHUDDER PHOTOGRAPHY

0521 **Topsy Turvy Design**, USA

PHOTOGRAPHY: JENNIFER LOVELY

0522 **Diana Vick**, USA

0523 **P.J. Pilgrim,** Apple Blossom Photography, USA

PHOTOGRAPHY: MARIA S. VARELA, SANTIAGO ALVAREZ

0524 **Penelope Almendros Garcia,**
Revue Vintage, Spain

0525   **Penelope Almendros Garcia**, Revue Vintage, Spain

PHOTOGRAPHY: R MARTIN ARMSTRONG

PHOTOGRAPHY: R MARTIN ARMSTRONG

0526 **P.J. Pilgrim**, Apple Blossom Photography, USA

0527 **Diana Vick**, USA

0528 **Diana Vick**, USA

PHOTOGRAPHY: SILENT SHUDDER PHOTOGRAPHY

PHOTOGRAPHY: SILENT SHUDDER PHOTOGRAPHY

0529 **Topsy Turvy Design**, USA

•----------► *0530* **Topsy Turvy Design**, USA

0531   **Topsy Turvy Design**, USA

0532 **P.J. Pilgrim**, Apple Blossom Photography, USA

PHOTOGRAPHY: DAVID TATE

0533 **Idris De Angeli, Zahira's Boudoir**, UK

0534 **Amy & Brayton Carpenter**, Legendary Costume Works, USA

PHOTOGRAPHY: DANIEL SILVEIRA

PHOTOGRAPHY: DANIEL SILVEIRA

0535 **Legion Fantastique**, USA

0536 **Legion Fantastique**, USA

PHOTOGRAPHY: R. "MARTIN" ARMSTRONG

PHOTOGRAPHY: MICHAEL PAO, MAD CALAMITY PHOTOS

0537 **Larissa Sayer**, Canada

0538 **Diana Vick**, USA

0539 **Lynda Taft**, USA

0540 **Erin Tierneigh**, USA

0541 **Erin Tierneigh**, USA

0542 **Erin Tierneigh**, USA

0543   **P.J. Pilgrim**, Apple Blossom Photography, USA

0544 **Martin Small**, UK

0545 **Lisa A. Rooney**, USA • - - - - ↓

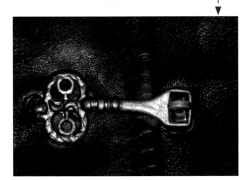

0548 **Lisa A. Rooney**, USA

0546 **Lisa A. Rooney**, USA • - - - - - ▶

0549 **Shirlene Perini**, USA

0547 **Lisa A. Rooney**, USA • - - - - ↓

0550 **Lisa A. Rooney**, USA

0551 **María S. Varela**, Model **Patricia Egea**, Clothing **Penélope Almendros**, Bavaria

0552 **P.J. Pilgrim**, Apple Blossom Photography, USA

0553 **P.J. Pilgrim**, Apple Blossom Photography, USA

0554 **Penelope Almendros Garcia**, Revue Vintage, Spain

0555 **P.J. Pilgrim**, Apple Blossom Photography, USA

0556 **Jessica M. Coen**, USA

0557 **Jessica M. Coen**, USA

0558 **Diana Vick**, USA

0559 **Diana Vick**, USA

0560 **Topsy Turvy Design**, USA

PHOTOGRAPHY: R. "MARTIN" ARMSTRONG

PHOTOGRAPHY: R. "MARTIN" ARMSTRONG

PHOTOGRAPHY: SILENT SHUDDER PHOTOGRAPHY

► *0561* **Topsy Turvy Design**, USA

0562 **Hilde Heyvaert**, House of Secrets Incorporated, Belgium

0563 **Hilde Heyvaert**, House of Secrets Incorporated, Belgium

0564 **Hilde Heyvaert**, House of Secrets Incorporated, Belgium

0565 **Hilde Heyvaert**, House of Secrets Incorporated, Belgium

0566 **Hilde Heyvaert**, House of Secrets Incorporated, Belgium • – – – – –

0567 **Hilde Heyvaert**, House of Secrets Incorporated, Belgium

0568 **Veronique Chevalier**, USA

0569 **Veronique Chevalier**, USA

●--► *0570* **Veronique Chevalier**, USA

0571 **Idris De Angeli, Zahira's Boudoir**, UK

PHOTOGRAPHY: DAVID ZENTZ

PHOTOGRAPHY: DAVID ZENTZ

0572 **Legion Fantastique**, USA

0573 **Idris De Angeli, Zahira's Boudoir**, UK

PHOTOGRAPHY: DANIEL SILVEIRA

PHOTOGRAPHY: AB MANN

PHOTOGRAPHY: DARKAIN MEDIA, WWW.DARKAIN.COM

0574 **Regina Davan**, Alt.Kilt, USA

0575 **Martin Small**, UK

0576 **Jazmyn & Logan Douillard**, Douillard Custom Creations, Canada ● ─ ─ ─

0577 **Michael Salerno**, USA

0578 **Deanne Smith**, Goldenthrush, USA

0579 **Jazmyn & Logan Douillard**, Douillard Custom Creations, Canada

0580 **Michelle Barton**,
Victorian Gothic Clothing, UK

●---► 0581 **Michelle Barton**,
Victorian Gothic Clothing, UK

0582 **Michelle Barton**,
Victorian Gothic Clothing, UK

0583 **Michelle Barton**,
Victorian Gothic Clothing, UK

0584 **P.J. Pilgrim**, Apple Blossom Photography, USA

0585 **Christine Jones**,
Crimson Chain Leatherworks, USA

0586 **Diana Vick**, USA

0587 **Diana Vick**, USA

0588 **Alison Park-Douglas**,
Velvet Mechanism, USA

0589 **Alison Park-Douglas**,
Velvet Mechanism, USA

0590 **Diana Vick**, USA

0591 **P.J. Pilgrim**, Apple Blossom Photography, USA

● - - ► *0593* **Pia Barile**, Pia Barile Accessories, The Netherlands

0594 **Pia Barile**, Pia Barile Accessories, The Netherlands

0592 **Jessica M. Coen**, USA ● - - - - ► *0595* **Jessica M. Coen**, USA

0596 **Jessica Faraday**, Faraday Bags and Bijoux, USA

0597 **Michael J. Marchand** and **Tim Marchand**, Ajar Communications, LLC, USA

0598 **Michael J. Marchand** and **Tim Marchand**, Ajar Communications, LLC, USA

0599 **Michael J. Marchand** and **Tim Marchand**, Ajar Communications, LLC, USA

0600 **Martin Small**, UK

0601 **Mike Jennings**, USA

0602 **Steve Ziolkowski**, Cinemagician, USA

0603 **Diana Vick**, USA

PHOTOGRAPHY: R. "MARTIN" ARMSTRONG

0604 **Mike Jennings**, USA

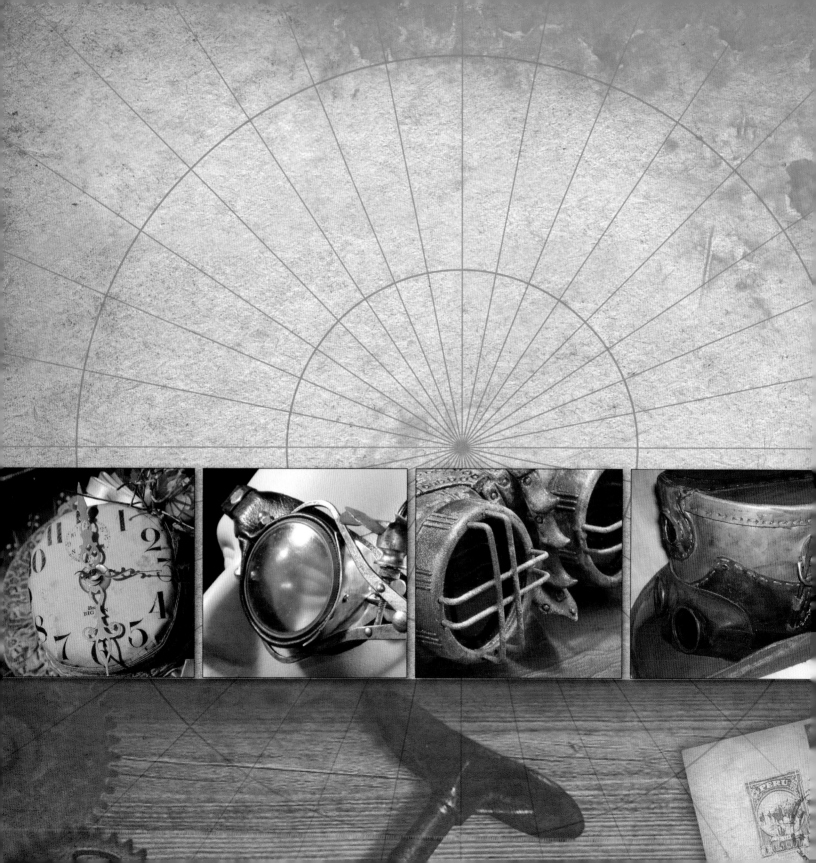

CHAPTER V:

HATS AND
ACCESSORIES

0605 – 0713 •••••▶

0605 **Cassandra Mathieson**, Cadaverous Lovely, USA

0607　**Melanie Brooks**, Earthenwood Studio, USA

0606　**Haruo Suekichi**, Suekichi Haruo Koubou, Japan

0608　**Dr. Grymm**, Dr. Grymm Laboratories, USA

0609 **q phia**, USA

0610 **John Paul Ammons**, Double A Stitching, USA

0611 **q phia**, USA

0612 **John Paul Ammons**, Double A Stitching, USA

0613 **John Paul Ammons**, Double A Stitching, USA

0614 **Abigail Cosio,**
Bedford Falls Headwear, USA

0615 **John Paul Ammons**, Double A Stitching, USA

0616 **q phia**, USA

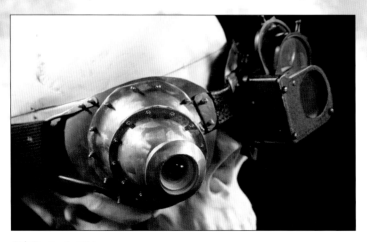

0617 **Davin White**, USA

0618 **Dr. Grymm**, Dr. Grymm Laboratories, USA

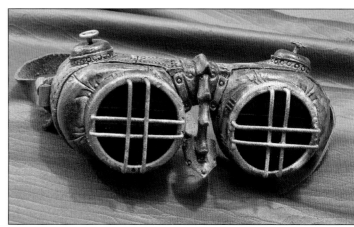

0619 **Dr. Grymm**, Dr. Grymm Laboratories, USA

•------▶ 0620 **Dr. Grymm**, Dr. Grymm Laboratories, USA

0621 **Dr. Grymm**, Dr. Grymm Laboratories, USA

•------▶ 0622 **Dr. Grymm**, Dr. Grymm Laboratories, USA

0623 **P.J. Pilgrim**, Apple Blossom Photography, USA

0624 **Emperor of the Red Fork Empire**, USA

● - - - - - - ▶ *0625* **Emperor of the Red Fork Empire**, USA

0626 **John Paul Ammons**, Double A Stitching, USA

0627　**Kat Fortner-McNiff**, USA

0628　**Kat Fortner-McNiff**, USA

0629　**Kat Fortner-McNiff**, USA

0630　**Kat Fortner-McNiff**, USA

0631 **Ramon R. Martin**, USA

0632 **Ramon R. Martin**, USA

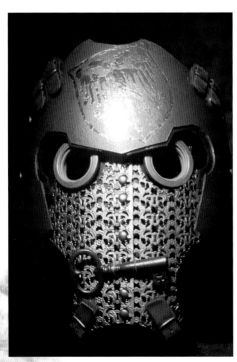

0633 **Eddie Wilson**,
whisperstudio broken toys, USA

0634 **Ramon R. Martin**, USA

0635 **Ramon R. Martin**, USA

0636 **Ramon R. Martin**, USA

0637   **Ramon R. Martin**, USA

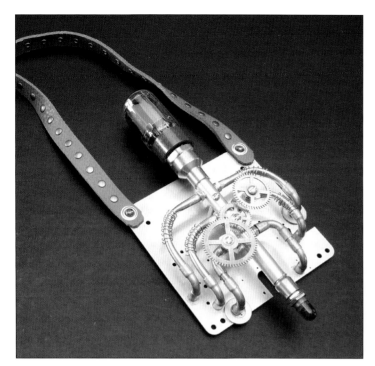

0638 **Thomas E. Gawron**, USA

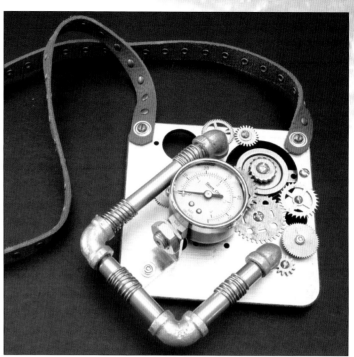

0639 **Thomas E. Gawron**, USA

0640 **Thomas E. Gawron**, USA

0641 **Thomas E. Gawron**, USA

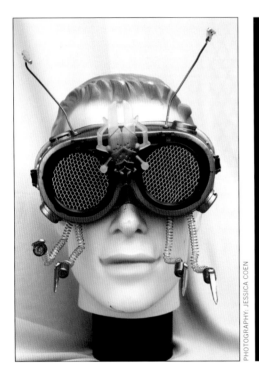

0642 **Emperor of the Red Fork Empire**, USA

0643 **Ian Finch-Feld**, Skinz N Hydez, Canada

0644 **A. Laura Brody**, Dreams By Machine, USA

0645 **Ian Finch-Feld**, Skinz N Hydez, Canada

0646 **Ian Finch-Feld**, Skinz N Hydez, Canada

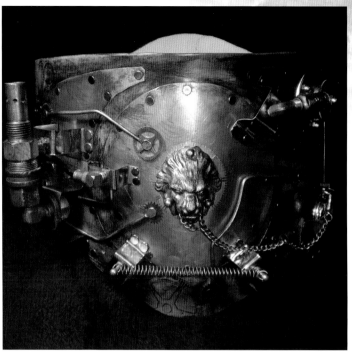

0647 **Ian Finch-Feld**, Skinz N Hydez, Canada

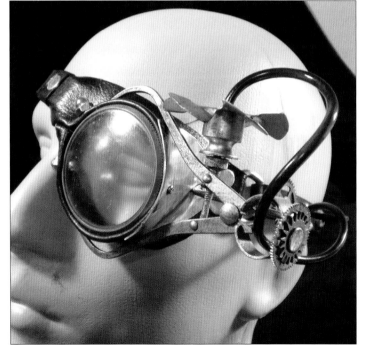

0648 **Ian Finch-Feld**, Skinz N Hydez, Canada

0649 **Ian Finch-Feld**, Skinz N Hydez, Canada

0651 **Ian Finch-Feld**, Skinz N Hydez, Canada

0650 **Ian Finch-Feld**, Skinz N Hydez, Canada

0652 **Ian Finch-Feld**, Skinz N Hydez, Canada

0653 **Ian Finch-Feld**, Skinz N Hydez, Canada

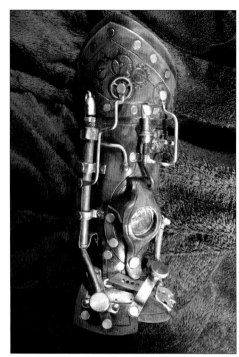

0654 **Ian Finch-Feld**, Skinz N Hydez, Canada

0655 **Ian Finch-Feld**, Skinz N Hydez, Canada

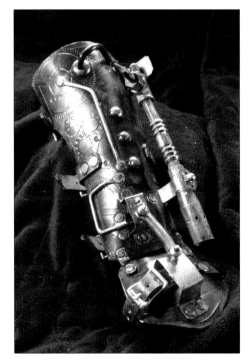

0656 **Ian Finch-Feld**, Skinz N Hydez, Canada

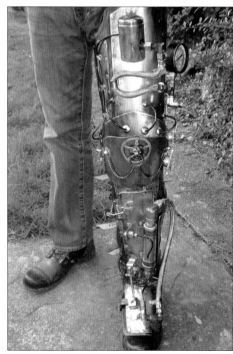

0657 **Ian Finch-Feld**, Skinz N Hydez, Canada

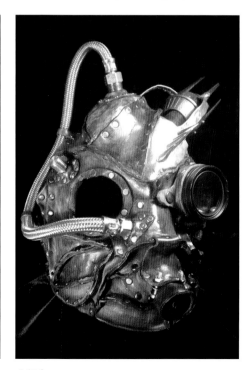

0658 **Ian Finch-Feld**, Skinz N Hydez, Canada

0659   **Ian Finch-Feld**, Skinz N Hydez, Canada

0660 **Ian Finch-Feld**, Skinz N Hydez, Canada

0661 **Ian Finch-Feld**, Skinz N Hydez, Canada

0662 **Ian Finch-Feld**, Skinz N Hydez, Canada

0663 **Ian Finch-Feld**, Skinz N Hydez, Canada

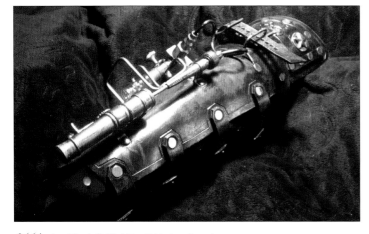

0664 **Ian Finch-Feld**, Skinz N Hydez, Canada

0665 **Ian Finch-Feld**, Skinz N Hydez, Canada

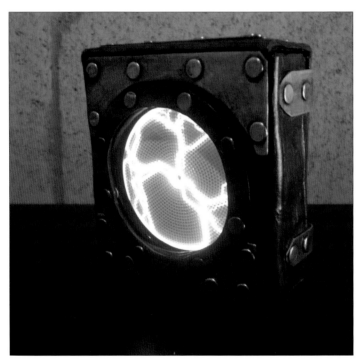

0666　**Ian Finch-Feld**, Skinz N Hydez, Canada

0667　**Ian Finch-Feld**, Skinz N Hydez, Canada

0668　**A. Laura Brody**, Dreams By Machine, USA

0669　**Isaiah Max Plovnick**, USA

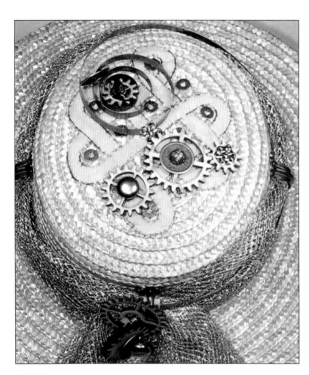

0670 **Heather Daveno**, Lao Hats, USA

0671 **Sheri Jurnecka**, Jurnecka Creations, USA

0672 **Cassandra Mathieson**, Cadaverous Lovely, USA

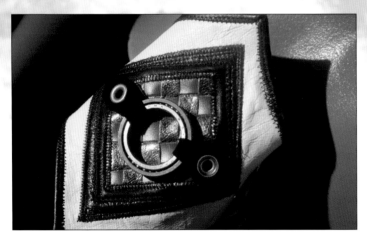

0673 **A. Laura Brody**, Dreams By Machine, USA

0674 **Matthew Borgatti**, Sleek and Destroy, USA ● - - - - - - ▶

0675 **Matthew Borgatti**, Sleek and Destroy, USA ● - - - - - - ▶

0676 **Matthew Borgatti**, Sleek and Destroy, USA

0677 **Heather Daveno**, Lao Hats, USA

0678 **Thomas E. Gawron**, USA

0679 **Thomas E. Gawron**, USA

0680 **Haruo Suekichi**, Suekichi Haruo Koubou, Japan

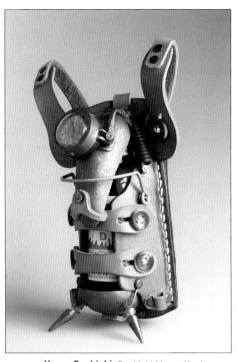

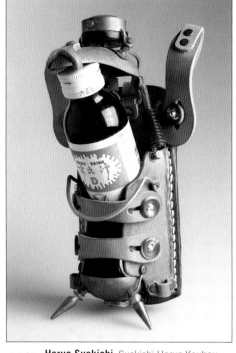

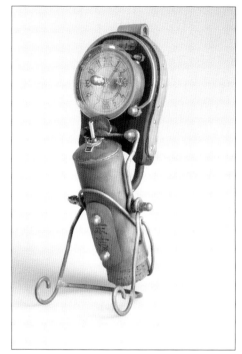

0681 **Haruo Suekichi**, Suekichi Haruo Koubou, Japan ●▶

▶ 0682 **Haruo Suekichi**, Suekichi Haruo Koubou, Japan

0683 **Haruo Suekichi**, Suekichi Haruo Koubou, Japan ▼

▶ 0684 **Haruo Suekichi**, Suekichi Haruo Koubou, Japan

0685 **Haruo Suekichi**, Suekichi Haruo Koubou, Japan

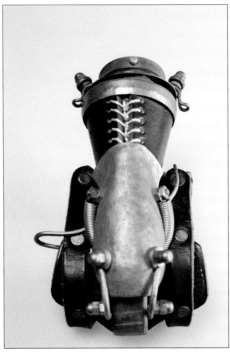

0686 **Haruo Suekichi**, Suekichi Haruo Koubou, Japan

0687 **Haruo Suekichi**, Suekichi Haruo Koubou, Japan

0688 **Haruo Suekichi**, Suekichi Haruo Koubou, Japan

0689 **Haruo Suekichi**, Suekichi Haruo Koubou, Japan

0690 **Jeffrey W. Lilley**, USA

0691   **Cassandra Mathieson**, Cadaverous Lovely, USA

0692 **Jessica Faraday**, Faraday Bags and Bijoux, USA

●------▶

0693 **Jessica Faraday**, Faraday Bags and Bijoux, USA

0694 **Abigail Cosio**, Bedford Falls Headwear, USA

0695 **Janet Teas**, USA

0696 **Heather Daveno**, Lao Hats, USA

● - - - - - - ►

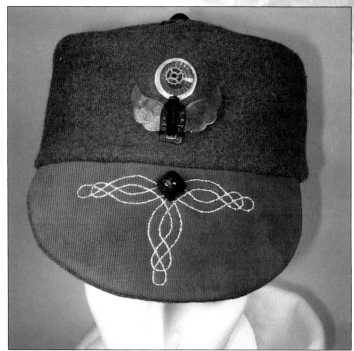

0697 **Heather Daveno**, Lao Hats, USA

0698 **Jessica Faraday**, Faraday Bags and Bijoux, USA

● - - - - - - ►

0699 **Jessica Faraday**, Faraday Bags and Bijoux, USA

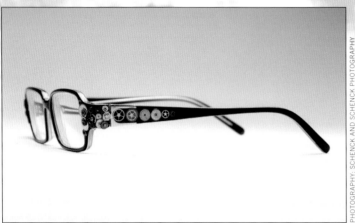

PHOTOGRAPHY: SCHENCK AND SCHENCK PHOTOGRAPHY

PHOTOGRAPHY: SCHENCK AND SCHENCK PHOTOGRAPHY

0700 **Terrill Helander**, Art My Way, USA ●- - - - - ▶ *0701* **Terrill Helander**, Art My Way, USA

0702 **Matthew Borgatti**, Sleek and Destroy, USA ●- - - - - ▶ *0703* **Matthew Borgatti**, Sleek and Destroy, USA

PHOTOGRAPHY: JESSICA COEN

PHOTOGRAPHY: JESSICA COEN

0704 **Emperor of the Red Fork Empire**, USA ●- - - - - ▶ *0705* **Emperor of the Red Fork Empire**, USA

0706 **Tom Banwell**, USA

0707 **Tom Banwell**, USA

0708 **Tom Banwell**, USA

•------▶ 0709 **Tom Banwell**, USA

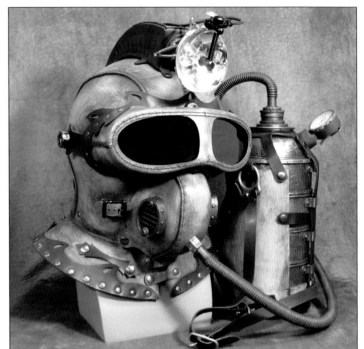

0711   **Tom Banwell**, USA

0710   **Tom Banwell**, USA

●------► 0712   **Tom Banwell**, USA

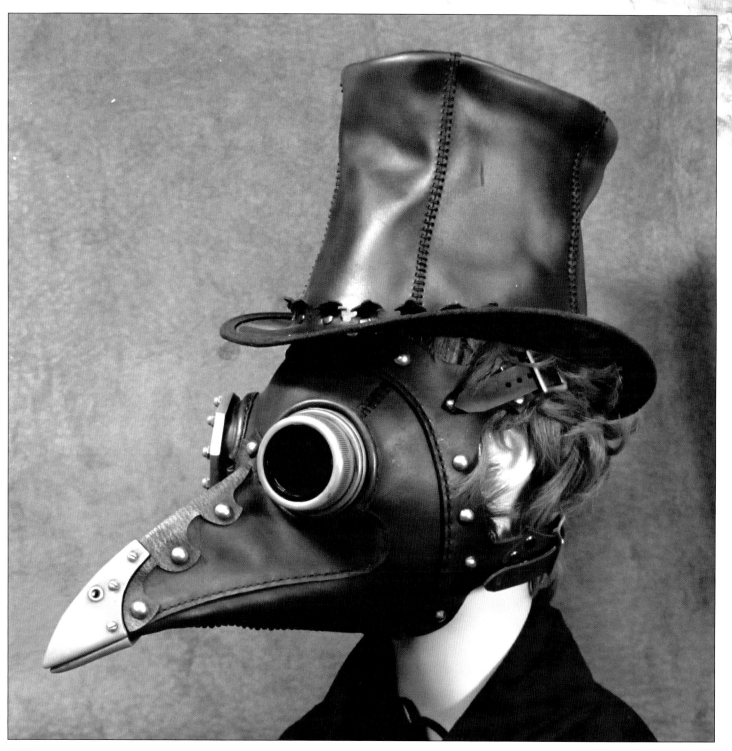

0713 **Tom Banwell**, USA

JEWELRY

0714 – 0870 •------>

0714 **Alison Park-Douglas**, Velvet Mechanism, USA

0715　**Christina "Riv" Hawkes**, USA

0716　**Billie Robson**, Art By Canace, USA

0717　**Christina "Riv" Hawkes**, USA

0718　**Christina "Riv" Hawkes**, USA

0719 **Karen Burns**, Vintage Findings, USA

0720 **Karen Burns**, Vintage Findings, USA

0721 **Karen Burns**, Vintage Findings, USA

0722 **Christina "Riv" Hawkes**, USA

0723 **Kristin Hubick**, Retro Cafe Art Gallery, USA

0724 **Kristin Hubick**, Retro Cafe Art Gallery, USA

0725　**Karen Burns**, Vintage Findings, USA

0726 **Jill Kerns**, Altered Ever After, USA

● - - - - - - ▶ 0727 **Jill Kerns**, Altered Ever After, USA

0728 **Jill Kerns**, Altered Ever After, USA

0729 **Jill Kerns**, Altered Ever After, USA

0730 **Jill Kerns**, Altered Ever After, USA •--►0731 **Jill Kerns**, Altered Ever After, USA 0732 **Jill Kerns**, Altered Ever After, USA

0733 **Jill Kerns**, Altered Ever After, USA

0734 **Sarah Stocking** aka Vespertine Nova Lark, The Spectra Nova, USA

0735 **Deryn Mentock**, Something Sublime, USA

0736 **Deryn Mentock**, Something Sublime, USA

● - - - - - - - ► 0737 **Deryn Mentock**, Something Sublime, USA

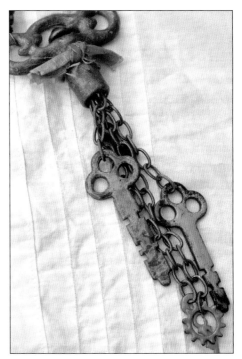

● 0738 **Deryn Mentock**, Something Sublime, USA

0739 **Deryn Mentock**, Something Sublime, USA

● - - - - - ► 0740 **Deryn Mentock**, Something Sublime, USA

0741 **Terrill Helander**, Art My Way, USA

0742 **Barbe Saint John**, Saints & Sinners, USA

0743 **Kecia Deveney,** Lemoncholy's Studio, USA

0744 **Kecia Deveney,** Lemoncholy's Studio, USA

0745 **Kendra Tornheim**, Silver Owl Creations, USA

0746 **Kendra Tornheim**, Silver Owl Creations, USA

0747 **Kendra Tornheim**, Silver Owl Creations, USA

0748 **Kecia Deveney**, Lemoncholy's Studio, USA

0749 **Kendra Tornheim**, Silver Owl Creations, USA

0750 **Laurel Steven**, Rueschka by Laurel Steven, USA

0751 **Deryn Mentock,** Something Sublime, USA

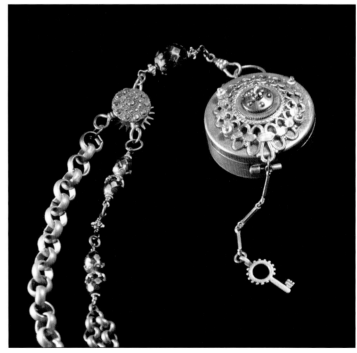

0752 **Angela Shaffer,**
Akeishaf's Fusion Fabrications, USA

0753 **Shawn M. Lopez**, USA

0754 **Shoshanah Jennings**, Adorning Erzulie, USA

► 0755　**Shoshanah Jennings**, Adorning Erzulie, USA

0756 **Tamara A. Mickelson**, T.M. Originals, USA

0757 **Tamara A. Mickelson**, T.M. Originals, USA

0758 **Matt Nyberg**, Leviathan Steamworks, USA

0759 **Tamara A. Mickelson**, T.M. Originals, USA

0760 **Matt Nyberg**, Leviathan Steamworks, USA

0761 **Matt Nyberg**, Leviathan Steamworks, USA

0762 **Matt Nyberg**, Leviathan Steamworks, USA

0763 **Matt Nyberg**, Leviathan Steamworks, USA

0764 **Brent Evan Scofield** a.k.a. Professor Quentin Zipcash, USA

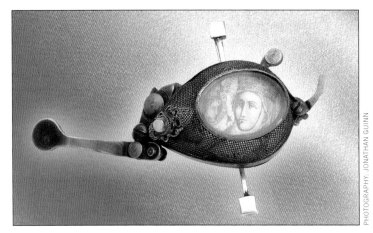

0765 **Brent Evan Scofield** a.k.a. Professor Quentin Zipcash, USA

0767 **Brent Evan Scofield** a.k.a. Professor Quentin Zipcash, USA

0766 **Jessica M. Coen**, USA

0768 **Jessica M. Coen**, USA

0769　**Billie Robson**, Art By Canace, USA

0770　**Shawn M. Lopez**, USA

0771　**Amanda Scrivener**, Professor Maelstromme's Steam Laboratory and Brute Force Studios, UK

0772　**Amanda Scrivener**, Professor Maelstromme's Steam Laboratory and Brute Force Studios, UK

0773 **InSectus Artifacts**, Australia

0774 **InSectus Artifacts**, Australia

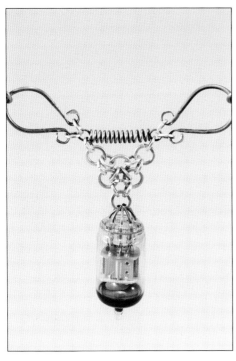

0775   **InSectus Artifacts**, Australia

0776   **InSectus Artifacts**, Australia

0777   **Amanda Scrivener**, Professor Maelstromme's
Steam Laboratory and Brute Force Studios, UK

0778   **InSectus Artifacts**, Australia

0779   **InSectus Artifacts**, Australia

0780 **Michael Thee**,
Michael Thee Studio, LLC, USA

0781 **Michael Thee**,
Michael Thee Studio, LLC, USA

0782 **Trisha Krueger**, MarySewDesigns, Germany

0783 **Trisha Krueger**, MarySewDesigns, Germany

0784 **Trisha Krueger**, MarySewDesigns, Germany

1000 STEAMPUNK CREATIONS

0785 **Trisha Krueger**, MarySewDesigns, Germany

0786 **Patricia Phillips**, USA •--► 0787 **Patricia Phillips**, USA   0788 **Patricia Phillips**, USA

0789 **Patricia Phillips**, USA •------------► 0790 **Patricia Phillips**, USA

0791   **Patricia Phillips**, USA

0792   **Patricia Phillips**, USA

0793   **Patricia Phillips**, USA

0794   **Patricia Phillips**, USA

0795 **Daniel Proulx**, Catherinette Rings, Canada

0796 **Daniel Proulx**, Catherinette Rings, Canada

0797 **Daniel Proulx**, Catherinette Rings, Canada

0798 **Daniel Proulx**, Catherinette Rings, Canada

0799 **Daniel Proulx**, Catherinette Rings, Canada

0800 **Daniel Proulx**, Catherinette Rings, Canada

0801 **Daniel Proulx**, Catherinette Rings, Canada

0802 **Michael Thee**, Michael Thee Studio, LLC, USA

0803 **Michael Thee**, Michael Thee Studio, LLC, USA

0804 **Michael Thee**, Michael Thee Studio, LLC, USA

0805 **Michael Thee**, Michael Thee Studio, LLC, USA

0806 **Barbe Saint John**, Saints & Sinners, USA

0807 **Barbe Saint John**, Saints & Sinners, USA

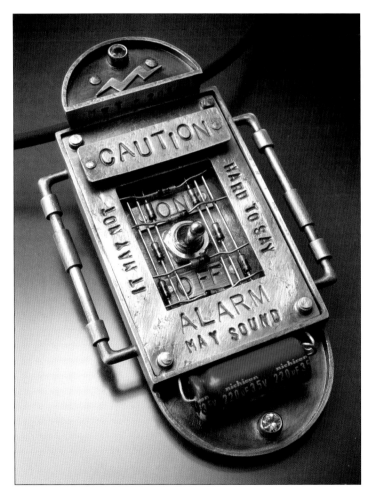

0808 **Michael Thee**, Michael Thee Studio, LLC, USA

• - - - - - - ▶ 0809 **Michael Thee**, Michael Thee Studio, LLC, USA

0810 **Daniel Proulx**, Catherinette Rings, Canada

0811 **Daniel Proulx**, Catherinette Rings, Canada

0812 **Daniel Proulx**, Catherinette Rings, Canada

0813 **Daniel Proulx**, Catherinette Rings, Canada

0814 **Daniel Proulx**, Catherinette Rings, Canada

0815 **Daniel Proulx**, Catherinette Rings, Canada

0816   **Daniel Proulx**, Catherinette Rings, Canada

0817   **Daniel Proulx**, Catherinette Rings, Canada

0818   **Daniel Proulx**, Catherinette Rings, Canada

0819 **Terrill Helander**, Art My Way, USA

0820 **Marina Rios**, Fanciful Devices, USA

0821 **Rainey J. Gibney**, The Josie Baggley Company, Ireland

0822 **Marina Rios**, Fanciful Devices, USA

0823　**Marina Rios**, Fanciful Devices, USA　　●－－－－－－－－－－－▶　0824　**Marina Rios**, Fanciful Devices, USA

0825　**Marina Rios**, Fanciful Devices, USA　　●－－－－－－－－－－－▶　0826　**Marina Rios**, Fanciful Devices, USA

0827 **Jane Salley**, USA

0828 **Kate Richbourg**, USA

0830 **Jane Salley**, USA

0829 **Jane Salley**, USA

0831 **Jane Salley**, USA

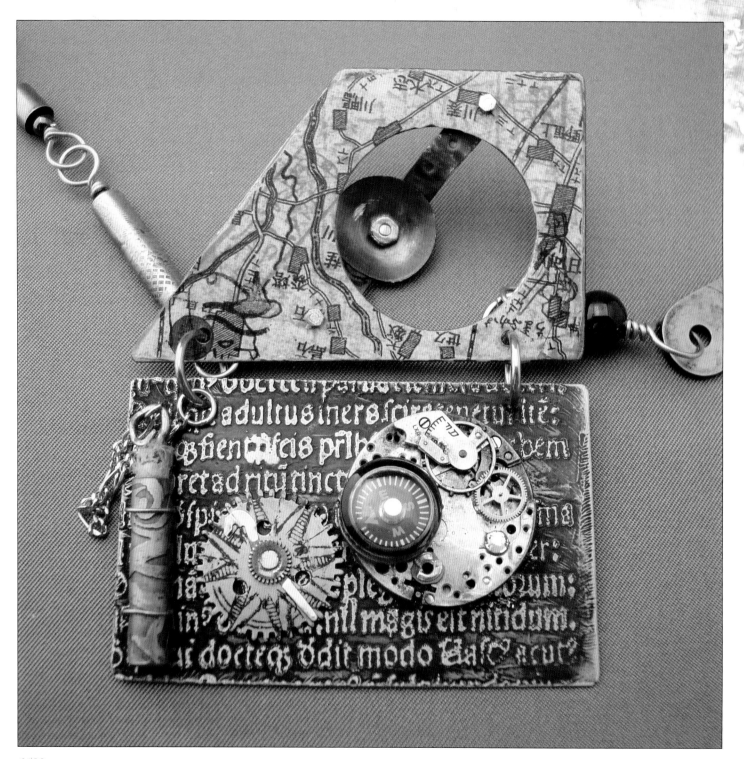

► *0832* **Jane Salley**, USA

0833 **Laurel Steven**, Rueschka by Laurel Steven, USA

0834 **Sarah Stocking** aka Vespertine Nova Lark, The Spectra Nova, USA

0835 **Sarah Stocking** aka Vespertine Nova Lark, The Spectra Nova, USA

0836 **Laurel Steven**, Rueschka by Laurel Steven, USA

0837 **Debbie Lynch**, USA

0838 **Debbie Lynch**, USA

0839 **Kerin Gale**, USA

0840 **Debbie Lynch**, USA

0841 **Jen Hilton**, USA

● ─ ─ ─ ─ ─ ─ ─ ─ ─ ─ ▶ *0842* **Jen Hilton**, USA

JEWELRY

257

0843 **Barbe Saint John**, Saints & Sinners, USA

0844 **Barbe Saint John**, Saints & Sinners, USA

0845 **Erin Keck**, E.K. Creations, USA

0846 **Erin Keck**, E.K. Creations, USA

0847 **Trisha Krueger**, MarySewDesigns, Germany

0848   **Christina "Riv" Hawkes**, USA

0849   **Alison Park-Douglas**,
Velvet Mechanism, USA

0850   **Alison Park-Douglas**,
Velvet Mechanism, USA

0851   **Christina "Riv" Hawkes**, USA

0852   **Cyndi Lavin**, USA

0853 **Sarah Stocking** aka Vespertine Nova Lark, The Spectra Nova, USA

0854 **Sarah Stocking** aka Vespertine Nova Lark, The Spectra Nova, USA

0855 **Alison Park-Douglas**, Velvet Mechanism, USA

0856 **Billie Robson**, Art By Canace, USA

0857 **Patricia Phillips**, USA

0858 **Sarah Stocking** aka Vespertine Nova Lark, The Spectra Nova, USA

0859 **Cyndi Lavin**, USA

●- - - - - - - -► 0860 **Cyndi Lavin**, USA

0861 **Cyndi Lavin**, USA   •‒¬

0862 **Cyndi Lavin**, USA   •‒¬

0863 **Sheri Jurnecka**, Jurnecka Creations, USA

0864 **Cyndi Lavin**, USA

0865 **Cyndi Lavin**, USA

0866 **Daniel Proulx**, Catherinette Rings, Canada

0867 **Daniel Proulx**, Catherinette Rings, Canada

0868 **Daniel Proulx**, Catherinette Rings, Canada

0869 **Daniel Proulx**, Catherinette Rings, Canada

0870 **Daniel Proulx**, Catherinette Rings, Canada

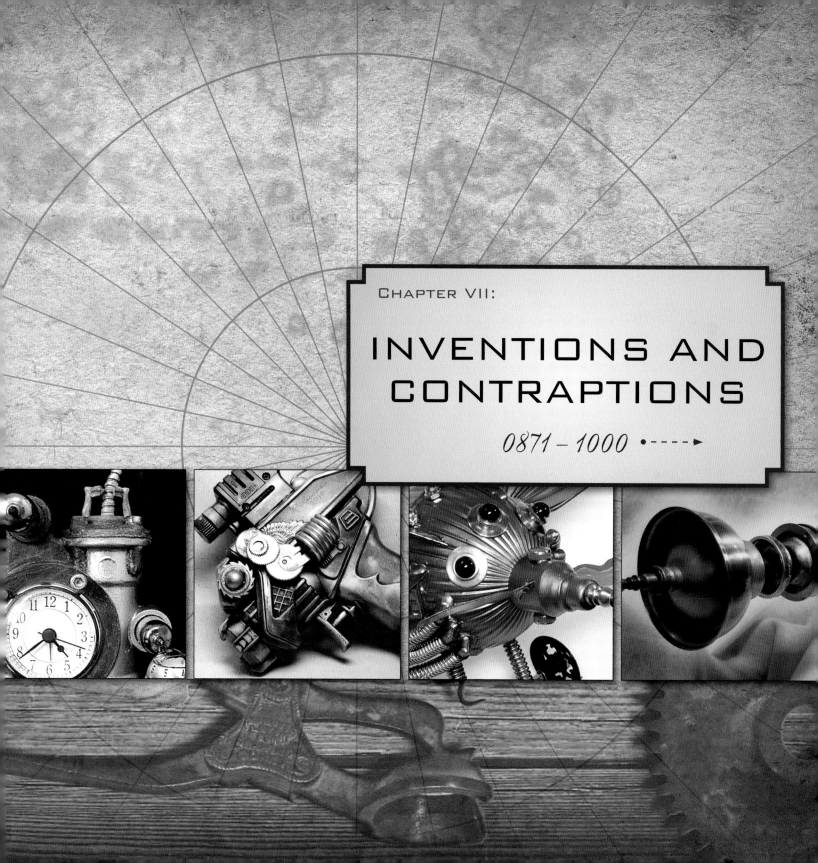

Chapter VII:

INVENTIONS AND CONTRAPTIONS

0871 – 1000 •·····➤

0871 **Brent Evan Scofield** a.k.a. Professor Quentin Zipcash, USA

PHOTOGRAPHY: JONATHAN GUINN

0872 **Eddie Wilson**, whisperstudio broken toys, USA

0873 **Brent Evan Scofield** a.k.a.
Professor Quentin Zipcash, USA

PHOTOGRAPHY: JONATHAN GUINN

0874 **Robert LaMonte**, USA

0875 **Brent Evan Scofield** a.k.a. Professor Quentin Zipcash, USA

0876 **Don Donovan**, USA

0877 **Don Donovan**, USA

●-----► 0878 **Don Donovan**, USA

0879 **Don Donovan**, USA

●------------► 0880 **Don Donovan**, USA

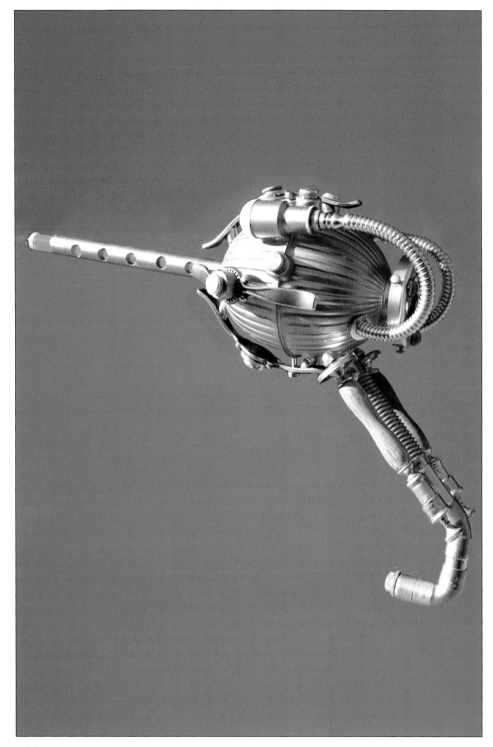

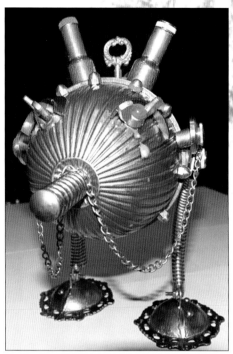

0882 **Don Donovan**, USA

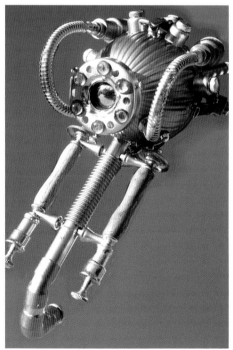

0881 **Don Donovan**, USA

• - - - - - - - - - - - - ▶ 0883 **Don Donovan**, USA

0884 **Jordan Waraksa**, USA

0885 **Jordan Waraksa**, USA •------

0886 **Jordan Waraksa**, USA

► *0887* **Jordan Waraksa**, USA

0888 **Jordan Waraksa**, USA

0889 **Jordan Waraksa**, USA

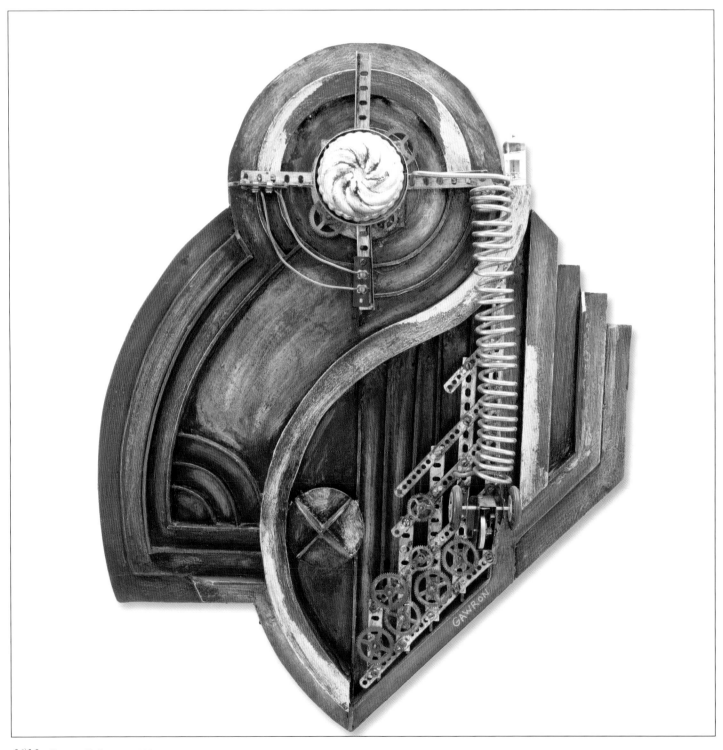

0890   **Thomas E. Gawron**, USA

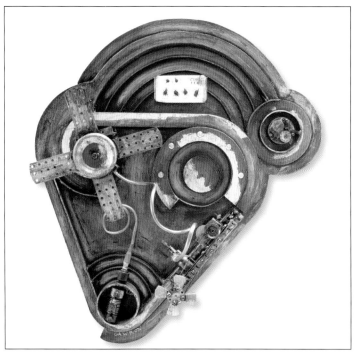

0891 **Thomas E. Gawron**, USA

0892 **Thomas E. Gawron**, USA

0893 **Thomas E. Gawron**, USA

0894 **Thomas E. Gawron**, USA

0896 **Daniel Valdez**, USA

0895 **Daniel Valdez**, USA

0897 **Daniel Valdez**, USA

0898 **Michael J. Marchand** and **Tim Marchand**, Ajar Communications, LLC, USA

0899 **Michael J. Marchand** and **Tim Marchand**, Ajar Communications, LLC, USA

0900 **Michael J. Marchand** and **Tim Marchand**, Ajar Communications, LLC, USA

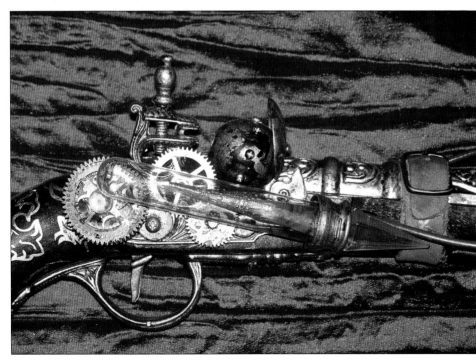

0901 **Eddie Wilson**, whisperstudio broken toys, USA

0902 **Eddie Wilson**, whisperstudio broken toys, USA

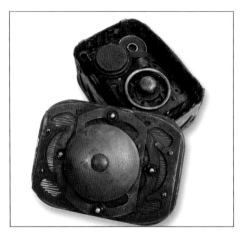

0903 **Urbandon**, Australia

• - - ► 0904 **Urbandon**, Australia

• - - ► 0905 **Urbandon**, Australia

0906 **Urbandon**, Australia

0907 **Urbandon**, Australia

0908 **Bruce Cooperberg**,
The Prototype Dept., USA

0909 **Urbandon**, Australia

0910 **Urbandon**, Australia

0911   **Jonathan Gosling**, River Otter Widget Studios, USA

0912   **K.Leistikow**, USA

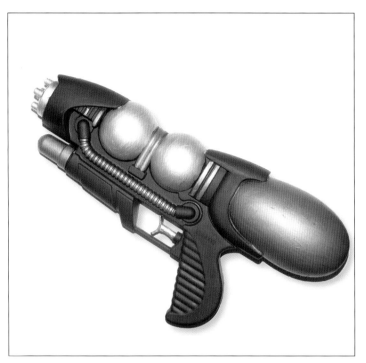

0913 **Lisa A. Rooney**, USA

0914 **Roger Wood**, klockwerks, Canada

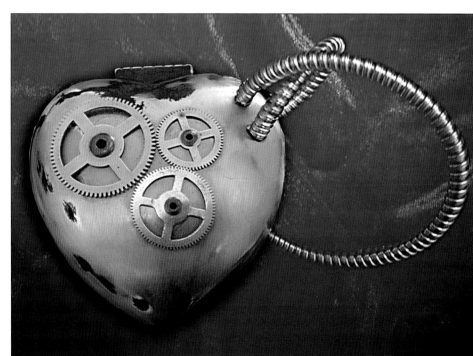

0915 **Jonathan Gosling**, River Otter Widget Studios, USA

0916 **Dr. Grymm**, Dr. Grymm Laboratories, USA

0917 **Stefan Stock**, Germany

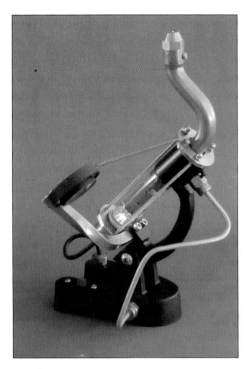

0918 **Stefan Stock**, Germany

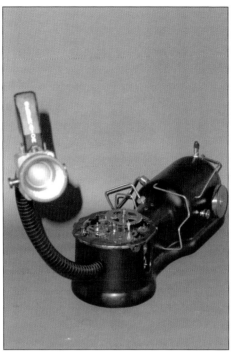

0919 **Stefan Stock**, Germany

0920 **Stefan Stock**, Germany

0921 **Stefan Stock**, Germany

0922 **Stefan Stock**, Germany

0923 **Tom Sepe**, USA

0924 **Tom Sepe**, USA

0925 **Tom Sepe**, USA

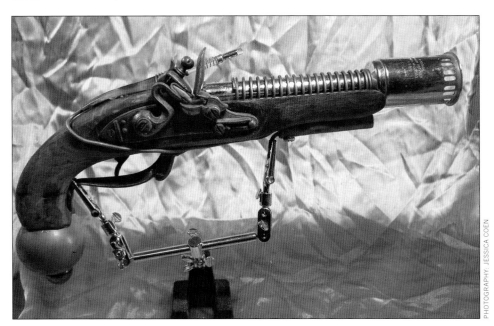

0926 **Boris Beaulant**, France

0927 **Emperor of the Red Fork Empire**, USA

● - - - - - - - - - - ▶ *0928* **Emperor of the Red Fork Empire**, USA

PHOTOGRAPHY: JESSICA COEN

PHOTOGRAPHY: JESSICA COEN

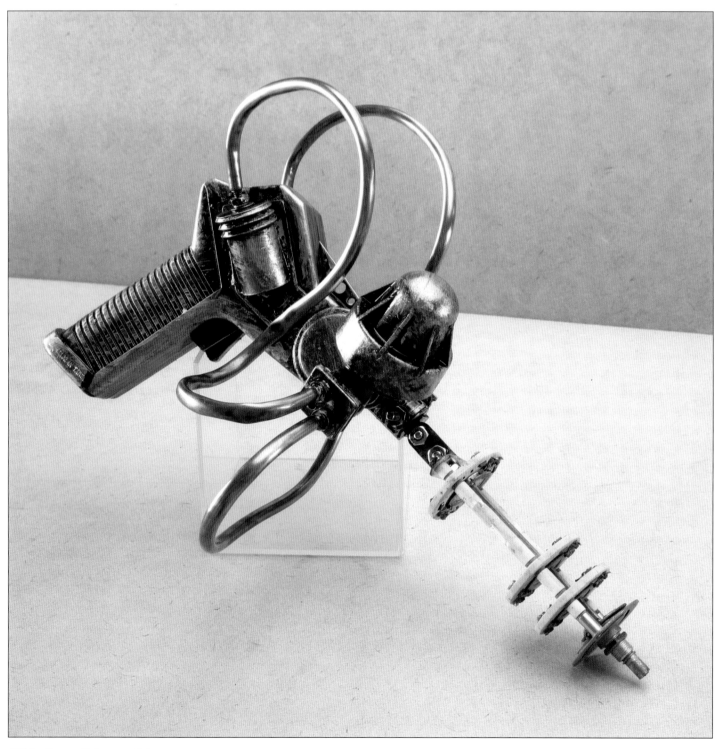

0929 **Thomas E. Gawron**, USA

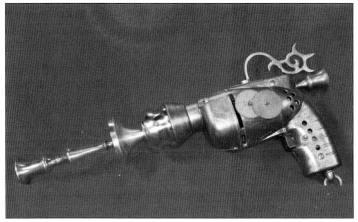

0930　**Jim Behrman**, USA

0931　**Jim Behrman**, USA

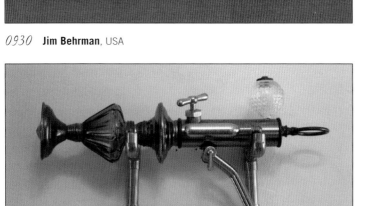

0932　**Christopher T. Coonce-Ewing**, USA

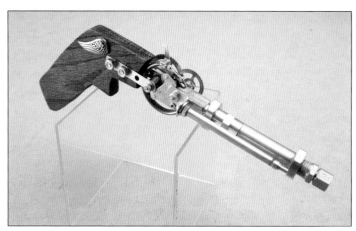

0933　**Thomas E. Gawron**, USA

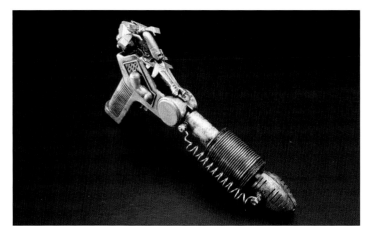

0934　**Thomas E. Gawron**, USA

0935　**Thomas E. Gawron**, USA

0936 **Steve Ziolkowski**, Cinemagician, USA

0937 **Michael Salerno**, USA

0938 **Steve Ziolkowski**, Cinemagician, USA

0939 **Dr. Grymm,** Dr. Grymm Laboratories, USA

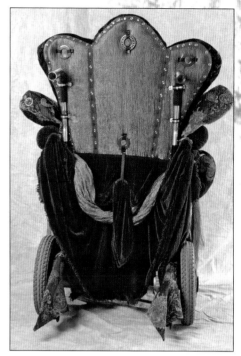

0940 **A. Laura Brody**,
Dreams By Machine, USA

● - - - - ▶ *0941* **A. Laura Brody**,
Dreams By Machine, USA

● - - - ▶ *0942* **A. Laura Brody**,
Dreams By Machine, USA

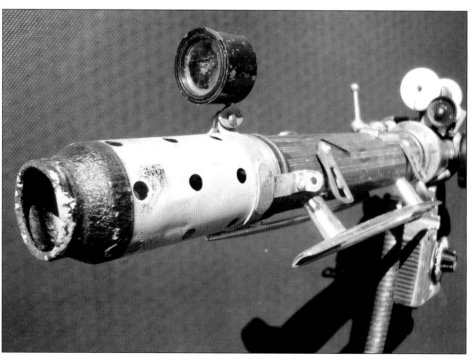

0943 **Martin Horspool**, Australia

0944 **Martin Horspool**, Australia

0945 **Robert Lucas**, Genuine Plastic, USA

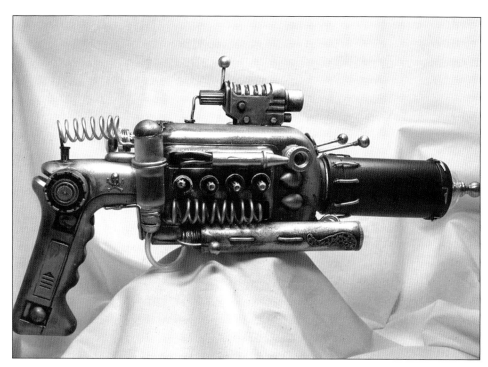

0946 **Robert Lucas**, Genuine Plastic, USA

0947 **Robert Lucas**, Genuine Plastic, USA

0948 **Robert Lucas**, Genuine Plastic, USA

0949 **Robert Lucas**, Genuine Plastic, USA

0950 **Robert Lucas**, Genuine Plastic, USA

0951 **Robert Lucas**, Genuine Plastic, USA

0952 **Robert Lucas**, Genuine Plastic, USA

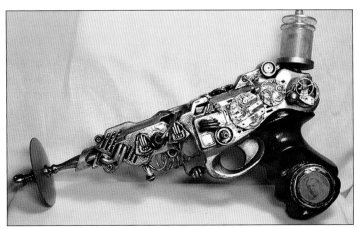

0953 **Robert Lucas**, Genuine Plastic, USA

0954 **Robert Lucas**, Genuine Plastic, USA

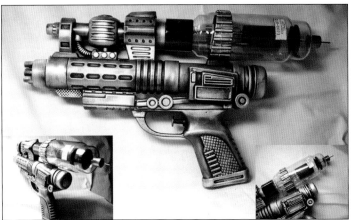

0955 **Robert Lucas**, Genuine Plastic, USA

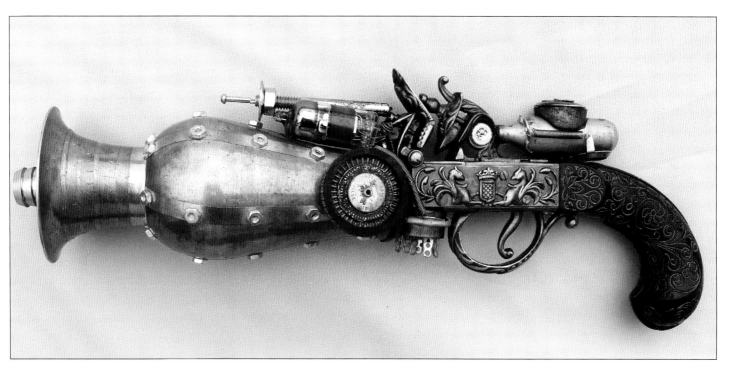

0956 **Sheri Jurnecka**, Jurnecka Creations, USA

0957 **Robert Lucas**, Genuine Plastic, USA

0958 **Sheri Jurnecka**, Jurnecka Creations, USA

0959 **Dr. Tony Valentich**, Australia ● - - ▶ *0960* **Dr. Tony Valentich**, Australia ● - - ▶

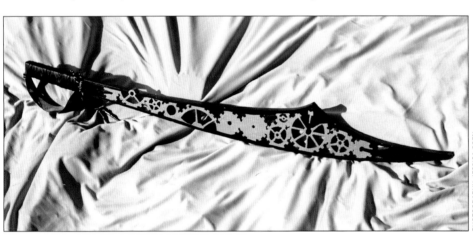

PHOTOGRAPHY: JESSICA COEN

0961 **Jeffrey W. Lilley**, USA

0962 **Dr. Tony Valentich**, Australia

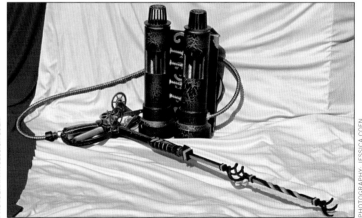

PHOTOGRAPHY: JESSICA COEN

PHOTOGRAPHY: JESSICA COEN

0963 **Jeffrey W. Lilley**, USA

0964 **Jeffrey W. Lilley**, USA ● - - - - - - - - - - - - -

0965 **Christopher T. Coonce-Ewing**, USA

0966 **Dr. Grymm**, Dr. Grymm Laboratories, USA

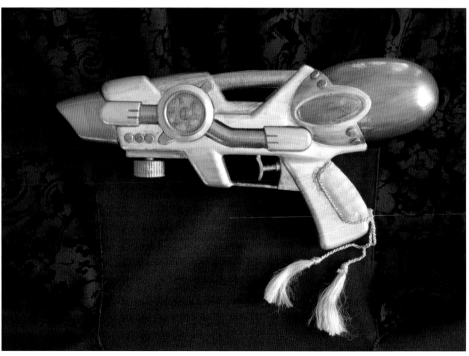

PHOTOGRAPHY: JESSICA COEN

0967 **Jeffrey W. Lilley**, USA

0968 **Larissa Sayer**, Canada

0969 **Dan Jones**, Tinkerbots, USA

0970 **Dan Jones**, Tinkerbots, USA

0971 **Dan Jones**, Tinkerbots, USA

► *0972* **Dan Jones**, Tinkerbots, USA

0973 **Anthony Jon Hicks**, Tinplate Studios, USA

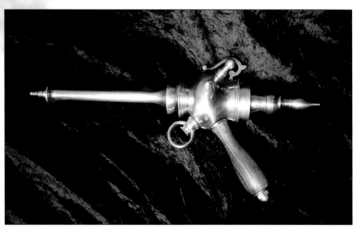

0974 **Anthony Jon Hicks**, Tinplate Studios, USA

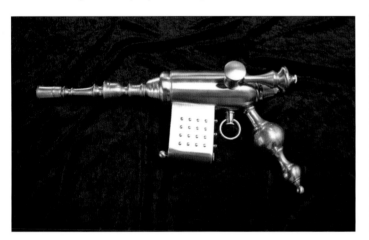

0975 **Anthony Jon Hicks**, Tinplate Studios, USA

0976 **Anthony Jon Hicks**, Tinplate Studios, USA

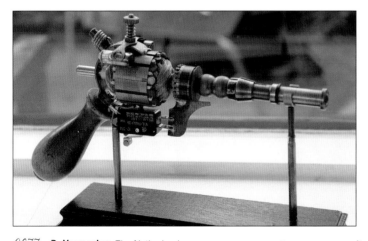

0977 **B. Vermeulen**, The Netherlands

●--------► *0978* **B. Vermeulen**, The Netherlands

0979 **Miriam Wilde**, USA

●- ► 0980 **Miriam Wilde**, USA

0981 **Miriam Wilde**, USA

●- ► 0982 **Miriam Wilde**, USA

0983 **Jon C. Acosta**, USA

0984 **Jon C. Acosta**, USA

0985 **Jon C. Acosta**, USA

0986 **Dan Jones**, Tinkerbots, USA

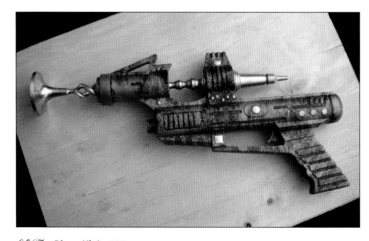

0987 **Diana Vick**, USA

0988 **Dan Jones**, Tinkerbots, USA

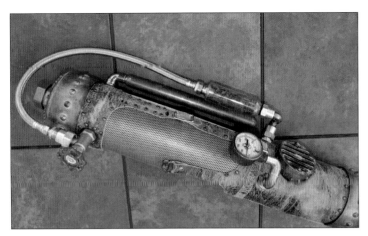

0989   **Steve Ziolkowski**, Cinemagician, USA

0991   **Steve Ziolkowski**, Cinemagician, USA

0992   **Dan Jones**, Tinkerbots, USA

0990   **Shawn M. Lopez**, USA

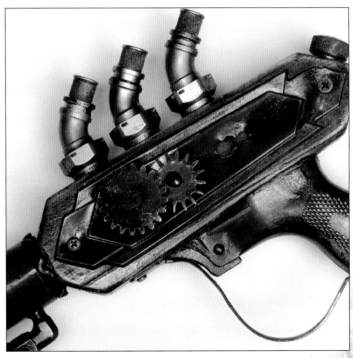

0993   **Dan Jones**, Tinkerbots, USA

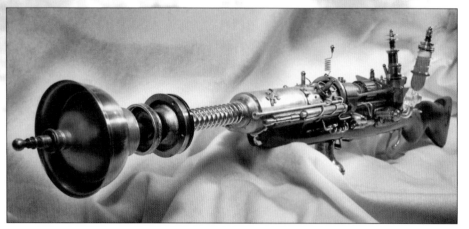

0994 **Allan K. Hunter**, Sirius Werks Phantasmic Phabrications, USA

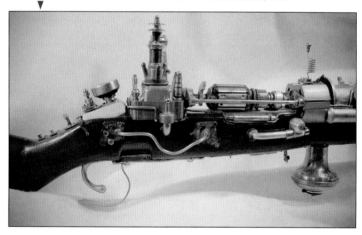

0995 **Allan K. Hunter**, Sirius Werks Phantasmic Phabrications, USA

0996 **Allan K. Hunter**, Sirius Werks Phantasmic Phabrications, USA

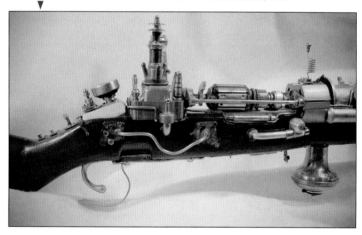

0997 **Allan K. Hunter**, Sirius Werks Phantasmic Phabrications, USA

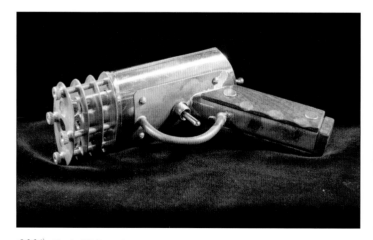

0998 **Davin White**, USA

0999 **Dr. Grymm**, Dr. Grymm Laboratories, USA

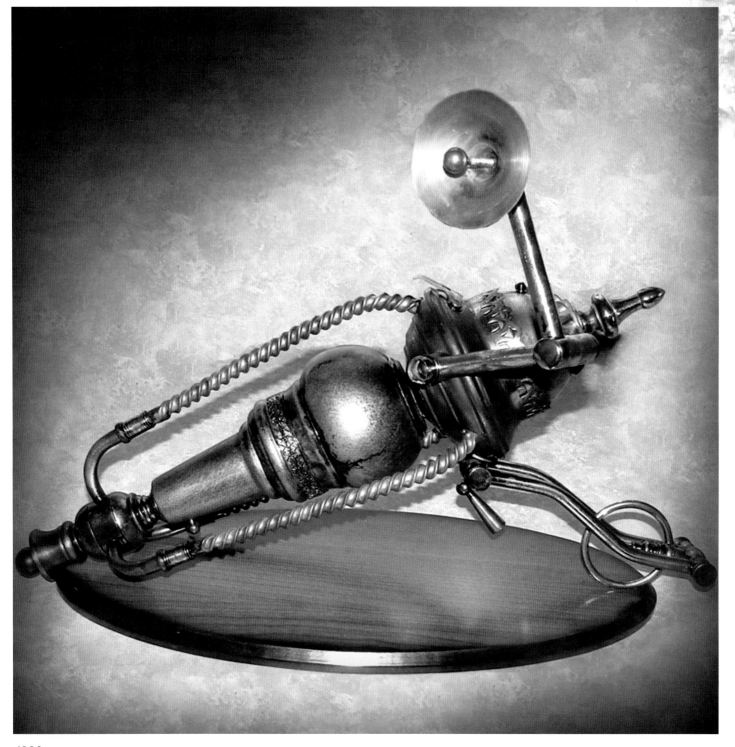

1000 **Dr. Grymm**, Dr. Grymm Laboratories, USA

IMAGE DIRECTORY

0001 Victrola Eye-Pod: iPod modified with brass, taxidermy eye, and brass horn

0002 detail of 0003

0003 Project #2: USB hub modified with brass, copper, and lead-free solder

0004 Project #3: USB hub modified with brass, copper, and lead-free solder

0005 detail of 0004

0006 detail of Victrola Eye-Pod

0007 Project #4

0008 Bellaphone 3: functional wooden speaker; can be connected with any device to fill a room with sound

0009 Electro-Voice Phenomena Recorder: functional EVP recorder with recording/playback mechanism and a frequency fluctuation detector

0010 detail of Electro-Voice Phenomena Recorder

0011 Thermo-Aether Meter: thermometer used to measure ambient room temperature

0012 Electro-Magnetic Frequency Detector: functional EMF reader with battery

0013 The Transportable Audionic Amplificator: portable Steampunk audio device

0014 The Professor Fang Self-Playing Bagpipe Guitar: guitar modified with found objects and leather

0015 detail of 0014

0016 Optiscope: assemblage

0017 MP3 Player Mod & Headphones Mod

0018 detail of 0017

0019 USB

0020 The Binagraph (Mark I): fully functional modern digital camera case

0021 Steampunk USB: 4GB USB drive with copper pipe fittings

0022 Telephone: assemblage

0023 Scorpion: modified USB drive

0024 Cthulhu: modified USB drive

0025 Time Machine: assemblage

0026 Mobile Phone: assemblage

0027 Blue Brass: modified USB drive

0028 detail of 0027

0029 Steampunk artifact

0030 Moonflower: modified solar lamp

0031 detail of 0030

0032 3000 Steampunk USB drive

0033 SteamPunker: full-size guitar made from wood and found objects

0034 found objects, mixed media

0035 detail of 0034

0036 Assemblage sculpture with found objects

0037 Steampunk Cellphone: Photoshop illustration

0038 USB Drive Mod: 4GB USB drive modified with brass, copper tubing, leather, and jewel pieces

0039 detail of 0038

0040 Steampunk Motorcycle: Photoshop illustration

0041 Steampunk VW Bug: Photoshop illustration

0042 Steampunk PSP: Photoshop illustration

0043 Love Song: black and white charcoal on tan paper

0044 Machine Head: graphite on paper

0045 See Horse: graphite on paper

0046 Elephant: graphite on white paper with digital distressing

0047 Graphophone Woman: graphite on coffee- and mud-stained paper

0048 The Sewing Machine Is Beautiful: black and white charcoal on white paper

0049 Shutterbug: graphite on cream paper

0050 Gramophone Man: black and white charcoal on white paper

0051 Mod Rocket: assemblage

0052 Steampunk Cake: assemblage

0053 Balloon Chariot: acrylic painting on masonite

0054 Anglerfish Submarine: acrylic painting on masonite

0055 Mechanical Angel I: acrylic painting on masonite

0056 Steampunk Seahorses: focal bead

0057 Steampunk Fish: focal bead

0058 Time Machine XXIX (Returning to White City 1893: Part 1): mixed-media painting with 3D sculptural objects

0059 Time Machine XLIX: mixed-media painting with 3D objects

0060 Sound Machine I: mixed-media painting with 3D objects

0061 Lord of Total Information Awareness (with Constitutional Reliquary): assemblage

0062 Reliquary for the Third Eye of William S. Burroughs: assemblage

0063 Cumulus Zeppelin: assemblage

0064 detail of 0063

0065 GreedEater: assemblage

0066 TriloTemporalis: assemblage

0067 detail of 0065

0068 Internal Combustion #2—Bone Machine: assemblage

0069 Factotum: assemblage

0070 detail of 0069

0071 Victorian Windup Toy Sculpture: resin, metal, and patina

0072 detail of 0071

0073 Duck: mixed-media assemblage

0074 Hallucination Engine: assemblage

0075 detail of 0074

0076 Iron Geisha: costumes and styling by Heartless Revival

0077 Curio Theatre's production of Shakespeare's *Twelfth Night:* Steampunk photo illustration

0078 Curio Theatre's production of Shakespeare's *Twelfth Night:* Steampunk photo illustration

0079 Curio Theatre's production of Shakespeare's *Twelfth Night:* Steampunk photo illustration

0080 Curio Theatre's production of Shakespeare's *Twelfth Night:* Steampunk photo illustration

0081 Curio Theatre's production of Shakespeare's *Twelfth Night:* Steampunk photo illustration

0082 Liza James & Jared Axelrod: Steampunk photo illustration

0083 Little Cable: mixed media/collage; Dresden scrap, found images and objects, cigar band

0084 Set Against Type: mixed media/collage; font exemplars, prepared papers, ticker tape, typewriter key, Dresden scrap, wire mesh

0085 Time Out of Mind: mixed media/collage; watch faces, watch hands, decorative brads, watch gears, prepared papers

0086 Bugbot #5: cicada shell in resin with assemblage, mounted on driftwood in a glass dome

0087 Bugbot #2: cicada shell in resin with assemblage, mounted on driftwood in a glass dome

0088 Curvaceous Steel: silver polymer clay with found objects

0089 E.S.T. Brain: sculpted polymer clay with found objects

0090 "Barbed Rosette" Industrial Heart #82: sculpted polymer clay with found objects

0091 "Aviator" Industrial Heart #84: sculpted polymer clay with found objects

0092 "Life with HLHS" Industrial Heart #77: matching anatomically correct sculpted hearts, polymer clay, and found objects

0093 "Curious Contraption" Industrial Heart #80: sculpted polymer clay with found objects

0094 Secret Garden: scultped polymer clay with wire and brass chain

0095 "Ocean Blue" Industrial Heart #75: anatomically correct sculpted heart, polymer clay, and found objects

0096 Deidrich—Mechanical Birdie V.2.0: scultped polymer clay with found objects and LED eyes

0097 "Eric's Heart" Industrial Heart #66: life-size silver polymer clay sculpted heart with found objects

0098 Mechanical Birdie V.2.0: sculpted polymer clay with found objects

0099 Mechanical Jellyfish: sculpted polymer clay with found objects

0100 Catacean Airship: watercolor painting

0101 Churning Back Time 2: Steampunk-inspired photography

0102 Peeping into the Past 2: Steampunk-inspired photography

0103 Peeping into the Past 1: Steampunk-inspired photography

0104 Churning Back Time 5: Steampunk-inspired photography

0349 Flood' Lamp: antique auto brake drum, plumbing, LED lights, and hand-sculpted solid glass drops

0350 detail of 0349

0351 Single on Wood: found wood, plumbing, LED lights, and hand-sculpted solid glass drops

0352 Gush Chandelier: plumbing and hardware, LED lightbulbs, and hand-sculpted solid glass drops

0353 detail of 0352

0354 Single Bronze Drip: recycled plumbing and hardware, hand-sculpted solid glass drops

0355 Blue-2-Drop: recycled plumbing and hardware, hand-sculpted solid glass drops

0356 Leak: recycled plumbing, hardware, wood, LED lights, and hand-sculpted solid glass drops

0357 Tide Chandelier: plumbing and hardware, LED lightbulbs, and hand-sculpted solid glass drops

0358 detail of 0357

0359 Dripping: plumbing, epoxy, and hand-sculpted solid glass drops

0360 Wave' Chandelier: plumbing and hardware, LED lightbulbs, and hand-sculpted solid glass drops

0361 detail of 0360

0362 detail of 0359

0363 Candles made from casting of impala horns

0364 assemblage sculpture

0365 assemblage sculpture

0366 assemblage sculpture

0367 assemblage sculpture

0368 assemblage sculpture

0369 assemblage sculpture

0370 assemblage sculpture

0371 assemblage sculpture

0372 Micron: welded metal lamp with glass globe

0373 detail of 0372

0374 Neptune: metal lamp with metal mesh

0375 Sandpiper: welded metal arm lamp

0376 Wall sconce I: wall lamp with metal mesh

0377 Table Lamp: plumbing hardware

0378 Steampunk Track Light: welded metal

0379 Victor: welded metal arm lamp

0380 detail of 0378

0381 Neophyte Thermo Indicator: brass and copper mounted on a solenoid base

0382 detail of 0381

0383 Trident Thermo Indicator: valved, welded, and screwed brass, and copper mechanical thermometer

0384 detail of 0383

0385 The Gentleman's Grooming and Information Station: Steampunk furniture piece with functional hot water, hair dryer, soap dispenser, tooth brush holder, false teeth tray, towel rail, bow tie hanger, and iPod holder

0386 Desk 2506: salvaged wood and swing bridge gears

0387 Muscatel Shelves: shelves reclaimed from a 20 foot (6 m) muscatel wine fermenting barrel

0388 Mantel Time Machine: mixed media, watch, and hardware

0389 Time Traveler's Journal: brass, watch parts, velvet, and assemblage

0390 detail of 0388

0391 detail of 0389

0392 Red Fork Empire journal: Handmade book with Red Fork Empire logo filled with tea-stained pages

0393 Bronze Set: recycled plumbing and hardware, hand-sculpted solid glass drops

0394 Fright Light: assemblage

0395 Steampunk Weber: fully functional redesigned Weber grill

0396 detail of 0394

0397 Steampunk Lamp: modified with found objects

0398 Fairy Lighthouse Lamp: smoke lamp made with liquid soap, assemblage sculpture inside

0399 detail of 0398

0400 detail of 0398

0401 assemblage sculpture

0402 assemblage sculpture

0403 assemblage sculpture

0404 assemblage sculpture

0405 assemblage sculpture

0406 assemblage sculpture

0407 assemblage sculpture

0408 assemblage sculpture

0409 assemblage sculpture

0410 assemblage sculpture

0411 assemblage sculpture

0412 assemblage sculpture

0413 assemblage sculpture

0414 assemblage sculpture

0415 Single-toggle switch plate: found objects

0416 Single-toggle switch plate: found objects

0417 Steampunk knob: found objects

0418 Two-Toggle light switch plate: found objects

0419 Steampunk knob: found objects

0420 The Pentarium Lamp: black walnut, various metals, mica, and acrylic

0421 detail of 0420

0422 detail of 0420

0423 The Braxtonian Lantern: handmade from metal and mahogany

0424 detail of 0423

0425 The Cylindrium Lamp: handmade of black walnut, mica, and various metals

0426 detail of 0425

0427 detail of 0425

0428 Steampunk Wall Clock: wood laser-cut gears, paint, antique clock and watch gears, found objects, lightbulbs, vintage tags, and discarded hardware

0429 Demon Lamp: copper, rawhide wings, and skull of a Florida land tortoise. The tail is from an armadillo.

0430 Steampunk Pendulum Clock: wood laser-cut gears, paint, antique clock and watch gears, found objects, lightbulbs, vintage tags, and discarded hardware

0431 Copper Journal: roofing copper, torch distressing, handmade hinges, antique door hardware and found objects, and handmade paper

0432 Copper Journal: roofing copper, torch distressing, handmade hinges, antique door hardware and found objects, and handmade paper

0433 The Orrery Chandelier: commissioned chandelier, parts hand fabricated from mild steel rod, flat bar, and sheet metal

0434 Steampunk Wall Clock: wood laser-cut gears, paint, antique clock and watch gears, found objects, lightbulbs, vintage tags, and discarded hardware

0435 detail of 0433

0436 Kaleidoscope 1: mixed media, brass candlestick, and clock parts

0437 detail of 0436

0438 Kaleidoscope 3: mixed media, brass candlestick, and clock parts

0439 detail of 0438

0440 Kaleidoscope 2: mixed media, brass candlestick, and clock parts

0441 detail of 0440

0442 Bible Cover for an Airship Chaplain: tea-stained canvas, moving gears, and wood rendering of gauge attached with metal rivets

0443 detail of 0442

0444 Nautilus Private Home Theater: based on the Nautilus sub from the Disney movie classic *20,000 Leagues Under the Sea*

0445 Nautilus Theater—Door

0446 Nautilus Theater—Wall detail

0447 Nautilus Theater—Diving Suit

0448 Steampunk Lamp: found objects, mahogany, and brass

0449 Wall Light: found objects, electron tube, and brass pocketwatch parts

0450 Steampunk Lamp: Dr. Lutra's Cure for Cadaverousness: found objects, gears, and lighting

0451 mural

0452 mural

0453 Triple-Toggle Switch Plate: found objects

0454 Four-Gang Light Switch Plate: found objects

0455 Steampunk Furniture Collection: infused with industrial fabrics and Victorian-inspired details

0456 The Saylor Cryptex: handmade vessel; combination lock box made of black walnut burl, brass, and synthetic ivory

0457 detail of 0456

0458 detail of 0455

0459 The Paradox Mouse: computer mouse, brass, and vintage typewriter keys

0460 detail of 0459

0461 detail of 0459

0462 detail of 0459

0463 Polymer Clay Box: embellished polymer clay

1000 STEAMPUNK CREATIONS

0672 Hats!: sewing, recycled bits and pieces from throwaway piles, and organic materials that were naturally harvested

0673 Xotique Wrist Cuff: repurposed leather jacket and purse with found objects

0674 Laser-cut leather goggles with brass goggles

0675 Laser-cut leather goggles with brass goggles

0676 Laser-cut leather goggles with brass goggles

0677 English Straw Steamer: straw hat embellished with found objects and lace

0678 Airship Pilot Equipment: assorted airship pilot accessories

0679 Airship Pilot: pilot costume

0680 Lunar Period: watch created with brass, leather, and wood

0681 Energy Drink: watch created with brass, leather

0682 detail of 0681

0683 Star Watching—Galileo: watch created with brass, leather

0684 detail of 0680

0685 detail of 0683

0686 Happy Cracker: watch created with brass, leather, springs

0687 detail of 0686

0688 Magical & Mystic Watch: watch created with brass, leather, wood

0689 detail of Happy Cracker

0690 Mono-goggle: welding goggles with leather and brass accents

0691 Clockwork: sewing, hat made with working clock parts

0692 Medic Bag: tea-stained canvas, silk, and wood cutouts

0693 detail of 0692

0694 Dyed feathers, hand-painted and treated leather

0695 Mini Top Hat: doll's felt top hat, feathers, tulle, and found objects

0696 sewing mixed media

0697 sewing mixed media

0698 Convertible Messenger-to-Clutch: brown denim with spray-painted appliques, screw-head rivets (regular and Phillips), and brass hardware

0699 detail of 0698

0700 Geared Up Glasses: watch parts, glasses

0701 detail of 0700

0702 Leather and brass goggles

0703 Leather and brass goggles

0704 Imperial Aviator Goggles: modified with found objects

0705 detail of 0704

0706 Firemaster: leather and resin gas mask and fireman's helmet

0707 Setinel: leather and resin gas mask, helmet, and gorget

0708 Rhino: leather and resin gas mask

0709 detail of 0708

0710 Pachydermos: leather and resin gas mask with copper auditory amplifiers; model carries a Raughnold raygun

0711 Underground Explorer: leather and resin gas mask, helmet, and goggles with a metal oxygen tank

0712 detail of 0710

0713 Dr. Beulenpest: leather and resin plague doctor's mask, leather top hat

0714 Mixed-media jewelrywork, wirework, and vintage watch movement

0715 Hammered, pierced, oxidized, and domed copper earrings; watch gears adhered via solder; wirewrapped labradorite briolettes

0716 Timeless: vintage optometrist lens, wirework, and watch and clock parts

0717 Post earrings: copper disc, ear wires, and soldered watch gears; oxidized with liver of sulfur and gently polished

0718 Hammered copper pendant with an old watch movement attached with a bezel setting

0719 Internal Workings: vintage watch parts, resin

0720 Key Details: vintage watch, frozen charlotte, and resin

0721 Unwound Charlotte: vintage watch, frozen charlotte, and resin

0722 Hammered, pierced, oxidized, and slightly domed copper earrings; watch gears adhered via solder; real beetle wings pierced with a pin and attached with copper jump rings

0723 Mixed media, vintage watch parts, resin

0724 Mixed media, vintage watch parts, resin

0725 A Girl and Her Bird: vintage watch, frozen charlotte, and resin

0726 I'm No Angel: cameo with vintage watch parts on a green and brown ribbon

0727 detail of 0726

0728 Cam: vintage hardware, cameo buckly

0729 384,403 Kilometers from Earth: watch face, vintage skeleton keys

0730 Odonata: vintage pocketwatch, chain, and glass

0731 detail of 0730

0732 Ask Alice: vintage keys, pocketwatches, and jewelry

0733 Fly: bracelet embellished with small gears

0734 Vintage watch parts, beads, and found objects

0735 detail of 0738

0736 Ornament: found objects, vintage watch parts, wire wrapping

0737 detail of 0736

0738 Touched: found objects, wire wrapping, and cold connections

0739 Steampunk with Color: found objects, sari silk, and enameling

0740 detail of 0739

0741 Tapestry Bracelet: sewn fabric collage, watch parts

0742 Clockworks: mixed media, vintage watch parts, and resin

0743 SteamPunk Watch. mixed-media jewelrywork, wirework, amd vintage watch movement

0744 Mixed-media jewelrywork, wirework, and vintage watch movement

0745 Bright Blue Leaf Clockwork Key: wire-wrapped antique key pendant with enameled copper wire, watch parts, glass, and Swarovski crystals

0746 Clockwork Key: wire-wrapped antique key pendant with enameled copper wire and watch parts

0747 Fire Spark Clockwork: wire-wrapped antique key pendant with handmade wire coils, enameled copper wire, watch parts, and Swarovski crystals

0748 Victorian Handcuff: vintage fabric, vintage doll, fabric collage, and sewing

0749 Wire-wrapped antique key pendant, silver-plated brass stamping, watch parts, and enameled copper wire

0750 In Memory of Dr. Mauser: hand-cast polymer clay, vintage watch, brass, and cold connection

0751 Reliquary Bracelets: found objects, vintage watch parts, and wire wrapping

0752 Steampunk Rosary: vintage watch parts, Swarovski beads, and crucifix

0753 Eight-Fold Amulet: copper, mica, and jewelry

0754 Aetheric Compass: mixed media, jewelry, vintage compass, and cold connection

0755 detail of 0754

0756 Reversible Compass Clockwork/Watchface Pendant: delica seed beads, recycled watch face

0757 Black & Gold Reversible Clockwork/Watchface Necklace: watch workings, delica seed beads, and Swarovski crystal beads

0758 Brass, epoxy, and wiring

0759 Asymmetrical Clockwork Necklace: watch workings, antique brass beads, and Swarovski crystal beads

0760 Clock face with epoxy, copper wire, leather, and re-created movement

0761 Clock face with epoxy, copper wire, leather, and re-created movement

0762 Various watch parts, lapis lazuli, and epoxy

0763 Various watch parts, lapis lazuli, and epoxy

0764 Tesla—P.E.T. Personal Electroshock Transmitters: assemblagc

0765 Brooch: assemblage

0766 Pin: fashion photograph of a handmade Steampunk pin

0767 Steampunk Personal Underground Radio Transmitter (S.P.U.R.T.): assemblage

0768 Ranks: photography of a portion of General Caled's Steampunk costume

0769 Spelling Bee: vintage brass, paper, and resin

0770 Sun Brass Heart: brass, copper, and sterling silver jewelry

0771 Opera glasses and chains

0772 Pocketwatch, pearls, and found chain

0773 Flux earrings #3: globes, steel, and sterling silver

0774 Industrial Necklace #8: ball bearing, bike sprocket, and steel

0775 Vacuum Tube Necklace #9: vacuum tube, hardware, rubber, and steel

0776 Vacuum Tube Necklace #10: vacuum tube, hardware, rubber, and steel

0777 Pocketwatch, quartz, and silver chain

0778 Roller Industry Necklace: roller bearing, bike chain, and steel

0779 Vacuum Tube Necklace #1: vacuum tube, leather, and steel

0780 Power: ring in sterling silver with blue sapphire and reclaimed steel bearing

0781 Northern Night: ring in sterling with 14k gold and rutilated quartz

0782 Attack of the Kraken Pocketwatch: Pocketwatch embellished with an octopus charm and vintage watch parts

0783 Pocketwatch Wings of Time: vintage pocketwatch clockwork embellished with a silver bird, set in a vintage pocketwatch

0784 Brooch: cameo with vintage watch parts on a green and brown ribbon

0785 Winged Hearts Necklaces: silver heart embellished with clockworks, rhinestones, wings, and watch parts

0786 Blooming Time Necklace: watch pieces, brass flower petals

0787 detail of 0786

0788 Royal Purple in a Timely Fashion Necklace: watch movement, chain, and beads

0789 Elgin Romance: old clock movement, purple pearl, and chain

0790 detail of 0789

0791 Paris Days Necklace: vintage pocketwatch, resin, and lace

0792 Torquoise Ribbon and Springs Choker: watch pieces, resin, lace, and beads

0793 Space and Time Necklace: men's watch, resin, and jewelry charms

0794 Romantic Red Necklace: clock movement, vintage jewelry, and chain

0795 Robot Ring: wire-wrapped robot ring with taxidermy glass eye

0796 Amber Ring with Clock Parts: ring with amber, clock parts, and copper

0797 GunMetal Ring: wire-wrapped ring with gunmetal copper

0798 Orange Reptile Eye Ring: wire-wrapped ring with orange taxidermy glass eye

0799 Arbor Amber Ring: wire-wrapped ring with clock parts inlaid in amber

0800 Lady Elgin Brass Bracelet: wire-wrapped bracelet with Lady Elgin Brass Pocketwatch

0801 Brass Scarab Bracelet: wire-wrapped bracelet with brass scarab stamping

0802 Star Bearings: ring in sterling silver with rhodolite, topaz, and reclaimed steel bearings

0803 Of Corset Matters: bracelet in sterling with 14k gold, amethyst, and sapphire

0804 Start Something: pendant in silver with 145 gold, copper, and kitchen match

0805 detail of 0804

0806 The Steam Engine Ring: soldering, found objects, and cold connections

0807 Time Machine Ring: soldering, found objects, and cold connections

0808 Alarm May Sound: pendant in sterling with 14k gold, sapphires, repurposed diodes, micro-switch, and capacitor

0809 detail of 0808

0810 Ring with Amber Eye: ring with taxidermy eye and copper

0811 Amber Ring: ring with amber, clock parts, and copper

0812 Ring with Gear: clock parts, copper

0813 Amber Ring with Clock Parts: ring with amber, clock parts, and copper

0814 Bracelet: brass, copper, and pocketwatch movement

0815 Ring with Lab Opal: silver, clock parts, and lab opal

0816 Bracelet: brass, copper, and pocketwatch movement

0817 Bracelet: brass, copper, and pocketwatch movement

0818 Bracelet: brass, copper, and pocketwatch movement

0819 Poe Bracelet: resin-coated image, watch mechanics, leather

0820 Ignorant Armies Antique Bulb Neck Piece: jewelrywork, assemblage

0821 The Navigator: found objects, resin, and wire

0822 Sacrificial Glass Fuse Assemblage Necklace: jewelrywork, assemblage

0823 The Chaldean Oracles Black Baubles Necklace: jewelrywork, assemblage

0824 detail of The Chaldean Oracles

0825 Stolen from a Tooth Fairy Lens and Tart Tin Reliquary: jewelrywork, assemblage

0826 detail of 0825

0827 Magic Window: etched copper, clock parts, and resin

0828 PMC Spinner Ring: cubic zirconia, silver, and rivets

0829 Secret Journey: etched copper, brass, clock parts, and miniature compass

0830 Captured Time: sterling silver bezels with watch and clock parts suspended in resin

0831 detail of 0829

0832 detail of 0829

0833 Scarlet Visions through Absinthe Eyes: hand-cast polymer clay, vintage watch, brass, and cold connections

0834 Vintage watch parts, beads, and found objects

0835 Vintage watch parts, beads, and found objects

0836 detail of 0833

0837 Man in the Moon: necklace made from pocketwatch body, embellished with brass and pewter charms

0838 Tick Tock Cuckoo: brass plate, wings, and charms

0839 Assemblage Pendant

0840 Time and Time Again: brass plate with watch gears and cogs

0841 Steam Faery: watch parts, brass wire

0842 detail of 0841

0843 Steampunk Reliquary Pendant: mixed-media assemblage, resin, found objects, and cold connections

0844 Dreams of Steam Necklace: found objects, resin, and mixed media

0845 Steampunk Key to Time Necklace: roofing copper, torch distressing, handmade hinges, antique door hardware, found objects, and handmade paper

0846 Copper Journal Necklace: roofing copper, torch distressing, handmade hinges, antique door hardware, found objects, and handmade paper

0847 Dream of the Kraken Necklace: octopus charm set on a black plastic filigree, embellished with vintage watch parts and black/violet flowers

0848 Sterling earrings, real beetle wings, and watch gears

0849 Mixed-media jewelrywork, wirework, and vintage watch movement

0850 Mixed-media jewelrywork, wirework, and vintage watch movement

0851 detail of 0848

0852 A Stitch in Time: faux leather created from felt, bead embroidery and basic wirework, ceramic bead

0853 Vintage watch parts, beads, and found objects

0854 Heavy Flight Pendant: vintage watch parts, beads, and found objects

0855 Mixed-media jewelrywork, wirework, and vintage watch movement

0856 Tres Punk: vintage metal parts, hand-forged iron setting, and hand-etched brass clock gear

0857 Cogs of Time Necklace: men's watch, resin, and found jewelry parts

0858 Vintage watch parts, beads, and found objects

0859 My Times Are in Your Hands: bead weaving and bead embroidery with mixed media

0860 detail of 0859

0861 The Dreamer's Chatelaine: faux leather created from felt, traditional and bead embroidery, basic wirework, eyelets, and chain

0862 Time to Run: mixed-media and chain necklace with cold connections

0863 Steampunk Chatelaine: assemblage, resin, wirework, copper foil, solder, beetle, vintage tools, and found objects

0864 detail of 0861

0865 detail of 0862

0866 Clock Gear Ring: wire-wrapped ring with clock parts

0867 Steampunk Amber Ring with Clock Parts: ring with amber, clock parts, and copper

0868 Steampunk Ring with Amber and Rutilated Quartz: ring with amber, rutilated quartz, and copper

0869 Brass Bracelet: wire-wrapped bracelet with pocketwatch movement

0870 Robot Beholder: wire-wrapped sculpture with clock parts and taxidermy glass eye

0871 Vintage C-GPS (Celestial Global Positioning System): assemblage

0872 Golden Lion Death Ray: assemblage sculpture

0873 Aether Spirit Containment Device: assemblage

0874 Steampunk Demonic Soul Retriever: plasma ball, recycled jewelry box, and assorted found objects

0875 detail of 0873

0876 Steampunkamobile: assemblage

0877 Time Machine: assemblage

0878 detail of 0877

0879 Steampunk Plane: assemblage

0880 detail of 0879

0881 Ray Gun: assemblage

0882 Alien Robot: assemblage

0883 detail of 0881

0884 The Ographer's Sundial: kinetic sculpture of recycled brewery parts, western red cedar, and brass

0885 Time Siphon: kinetic sculpture of recycled brewery parts, western red cedar, and brass

0886 Solunette: kinetic sculpture of recycled brewery parts, western red cedar, and brass

0887 detail of 0885

0888 The Oculist's Porthole: kinetic sculpture of recycled brewery parts, western red cedar, and brass

0889 detail of 0886

0890 Zephyr Ratio: interactive windup wall art combining wood and metals; each piece has movable parts

0891 Ulta Meter: interactive windup wall art combining wood and metals; each piece has movable parts

0892 Electro Shock: interactive windup wall art combining wood and metals; each piece has movable parts

0893 Quark Distiller: interactive, free-standing art combining wood and metals; each piece has movable parts

0894 Time Relay: interactive, free-standing art combining wood and metals; each piece has movable parts

0895 Steampunk Professor X Wheelchair: Victorian rocking chair built onto power wheelchair base with control panel, smoke, and sound effects

0896 detail of 0895

0897 detail of 0895

0898 Prediction Movie Machine: assemblage foley machine with mounted poster

0899 Steam-Driven Movie Machine: assemblage foley machine with mounted poster

0900 Fate of Icarus Movie Machine and Steampunk Coat Rack: assemblage foley machine with mounted poster

0901 Blueblood: modified flintlock pistol with found object embellishments

0902 Broken Heart: polymer clay with found object embellishment

0903 Communicator: assemblage

0904 detail of 0903

0905 detail of 0903

0906 Desktop Time Machine: assemblage

0907 Time Machine: assemblage

0908 Specimen Stand: wood, brass, and found objects

0909 Handheld Time Machine: assemblage

0910 detail of 0909

0911 Into the Aether: gearbox, metals, conduit, and found objects

0912 Fang Extractor: assemblage of found objects

0913 Steampunk Weapon

0914 Assemblage sculpture using found objects

0915 Steampunk Heart Jewelry Box: mixed metals, conduit, felt, rivets, and gears

0916 Vampyr Blood Transfuser: wood, glass, and rubber tubing

0917 Transformer housing with globe lamp attached

0918 Microscope base with electronic valve, LED-lighted

0919 assemblage

0920 Base of an old galvanometer combined with a flow meter and some plumbing parts, LED-lighted

0921 Cast-iron housing with electronic valves, LED-lighted

0922 Cast-iron housing of an old water pump combined with an old wall lamp; valve handle serves as switch

0923 The Whirlygig Emoto: an electric motorcyle with working steamboiler and room for three

0924 detail of 0923

0925 detail of 0923

0926 Zelo: wooden three-wheeled recumbent trike, beech

0927 Flintlock Essence Extirpator: assemblage sculpture using found objects

0928 detail of 0927

0929 Stream Electro Blaster: 1960s raygun modified with old plumbing parts and copper tubing

0930 Steampunk Raygun 2: assemblage sculpture using found objects

0931 Steampunk Raygun 1: assemblage sculpture using found objects

0932 The Regulator: assemblage weapon

0933 Airship Pirate Helium Ray: Steampunk raygun made from clockwork parts and brass pieces

0934 Battle-damaged Triconian Blaster: 1960s raygun with applications of transformer pieces and old radio parts

0935 Gatling Steampunk Torch: 1930s blowtorch with brass tubing and old clock gears

0936 Hypatia Ship: digital rendering of a Steampunk airship

0937 The Pentacycle: fully functional five-wheeled vehicle ideal for use by persons with balance issues

0938 detail of 0937

0939 Amelia Earhart Navigational System: antique radio housing with found obejcts and voice recording

0940 The Edwardian Cyborg Wheelchair: electric wheelchair with recycled sofa, drapery, and clothing fashioning the seats

0941 detail of 0940

0942 detail of 0940

0943 Raygun: assemblage

0944 Raygun 2: assemblage

0945 Little Brute GP_J7XT: assemblage

0946 GP011X Altara Plasma Manipulator: assemblage

0947 detail of 0946

0948 B. Rogers Raygun 001X: assemblage

0949 detail of 0948

0950 GP013X Green Laser Disruptor: assemblage

0951 Longfellow's Devastator: assemblage

0952 H. Solo Rapid Fire KD1911: assemblage

0953 Fitzgerald's Cosmic Ray Agitator: assemblage

0954 Buntline Astro: assemblage

0955 Electrotomic Manipulator: assemblage

0956 Raygun Bat-o-Matic 7000: assemblage, metalwork, replica flintlock firearm, brass vase, found objects, vintage radio parts, hardware, and adhesives

0957 GP004 Atomic Disabler (Pocket Gun): assemblage

0958 detail of 0956

0959 Jet Pack Bike: Steampunk transportation device

0960 detail of 0959

0961 Sword of Time: wood, brass sword

0962 detail of 0959

0963 Pistol made from saw handles and found objects

0964 Power Pack Gun: assemblage

0965 The Abrogator: assemblage weapon

0966 N20 Blunderbuss: wooden barrel, found objects

0967 detail of 0964

0968 Steam Pistol: modified water pistol embellished with paint, rivets, gears, and leather

0969 Steampunk Raygun: assemblage sculpture

0970 Steampunk Gun: assemblage sculpture

0971 Steampunk Weapon: assemblage sculpture

0972 detail of 0971

0973 Aetherlung Mark II: cold assembly sculpture

0974 Dumas Beam Pistol: cold assembly sculpture

0975 Blohm Gravitic Machine Pistol: cold assembly sculpture

0976 Maverick Plasma Pistol: cold assembly sculpture

0977 Found objects from household sources

0978 Found objects from household sources

0979 Revolving Incandescent Pepperbox Field Blaster: assemblage

0980 detail of 0979

0981 Reverse Paramagnetic Molecular Equilibrium Safety Pistol: assemblage

0982 detail of 0981

0983 Lumen Ex Consilium: light saber assembled from found objects, brass, and aluminium

0984 detail of 0983

0985 detail of 0983

0986 Zenith Electroblast: assemblage sculpture

0987 Suffragette: modified prop

0988 Pneumatic Aethier Disperser: assemblage sculpture

0989 Lunar Rebreather: Steampunk movie prop

0990 Your Wicked Future: copper, nickel silver, crystal ball

0991 detail of 0989

0992 Spitfire: assemblage sculpture

0993 detail of 0992

0994 De-Phlognosticator: found objects from household sources

0995 detail of 0994

0996 Flabbergastric Intesinnihilator (AKA "The Vengeful Monty"): found objects from household sources

0997 detail of 0994

0998 Violet Violence: wood, copper, LED lights, and lasers

0999 Proton Fundoplicator: found objects

1000 Echo Steam One: found objects, wooden base

ARTIST DIRECTORY

Jon C. Acosta, USA
jon.c.acosta@gmail.com
www.jonacodesigns.com
0983–0985

Mark E. Adams and Journeyman, USA
t12055@hotmail.com
www.myspace.com/
markadamssounddesign
0226

John Paul Ammons, Double A Stitching, USA
doubleastitching@gmail.com
doubleastitching.etsy.com
0610, 0612, 0613, 0615, 0626

Judy A. Anderson, USA
andersnr@centurytel.net
0211–0213

Joanne Archer, The Crow Road, UK
joanne_archer@btinternet.com
www.jo-crowroad.blogspot.com
0286

Azirca, New Zealand
speakwithoutmyvoice.blogspot.com
0034, 0035, 0243–0249

Tom Banwell, USA
tom@tombanwell.com
www.tombanwell.com
0706–0713

Pia Barile, Pia Barile Accessories, The Netherlands
pia@piabarile.com
www.piabarile.etsy.com
0593, 0594

Cory Barkman, Canada
cory.barkman@gmail.com
www.corybarkman.com
0372–0380

Michelle Barton, Victorian Gothic Clothing, UK
contact@victorian-gothic.co.uk
www.victorian-gothic.co.uk
0580–0583

Boris Beaulant, France
bo@borisbeaulant.com
www.borisbeaulant.com
0926

Jasmine Becket-Griffith, USA
jasminetoad@aol.com
www.strangeling.com
0053–0055

Jim Behrman, USA
jbb1972@sbcglobal.net
0930, 0931

Sandi Billingsley, USA
sandi@studiosandi.com
www.studiosandi.com
0241

Matthew Borgatti, Sleek and Destroy, USA
m@sinbox.org
www.sinbox.org
0311, 0363, 0674–0676, 0702, 0703

Jason Brammer, USA
jasonbrammer@mac.com
www.jasonbrammer.com
0058–0060

A. Laura Brody, Dreams By Machine, USA
laurabrody@verizon.net
www.dreamsbymachine.com
0644, 0668, 0673, 0940–0942

Melanie Brooks, Earthenwood Studio, USA
earthenwood@gmail.com
www.earthenwoodstudio.com
0607

Karen Burns, Vintage Findings, USA
vintagefindings@me.com
web.me.com/vintagefindings
0719–0721, 0725

Melissa Capyk, Wild Cakes, Canada
melc@wildcakes.ca
wildcakes.ca
0240

Amy & Brayton Carpenter, Legendary Costume Works, USA
amelobug@yahoo.com
www.legendarycostumeworks.com
0534

Kyle Cassidy, USA
kyle@kylecassidy.com
www.kylecassidy.com
0076–0082

Christine Cavataio, USA
ccavatai@yahoo.com
www.lunashowcasedesign.com
0415–0419, 0453, 0454

Chadwick, Australia
absurdabstraction@gmail.com
chadwick001.deviantart.com
0071, 0072

Tessa J. Chandler, USA
tessachandler@gmail.com
www.tessachandler.com
0470, 0471

Veronique Chevalier, USA
veroniquechevalier@gmail.com
weirdval.com
0568–0570

Tanya Clarke, Liquid Light, USA
tanyacclarke@yahoo.com
www.liquidlightsite.com
0340, 0341, 0343, 0349–0362, 0393, 0465

Mike Cochran, USA
mike@coppersteam.com
www.coppersteam.com
0183–0188

Jessica M. Coen, USA
altertheearth@gmail.com
jmcoen.deviantart.com
0151, 0153, 0556, 0557, 0592, 0595, 0766, 0768

Christopher T. Coonce-Ewing, USA
coonceewing@gmail.com
0932, 0965

NG Coonce-Ewing, Cricket Creations, USA
ngcoonceewing@gmail.com
ngcoonceewing.com
0216–0221, 0228, 0394, 0396

Kevin C. Cooper, Steampunk Kaleidoscopes, UK
kevin@steampunkkaleidoscopes.com
www.steampunkkaleidoscopes.com
0436–0441

Bruce Cooperberg, The Prototype Dept., USA
cooperberg@att.net
0908

Abigail Cosio, Bedford Falls Headwear, USA
bedfordfallsheadwear@gmail.com
www.bedfordfallsheadwear.com
0614, 0694

Derrick Culligan, USA
thesteamworkshop@gmail.com
thesteamworkshop.com
0002–0005, 0007

Regina Davan, Alt.Kilt, USA
techdragon@altkilt.com
www.altkilt.com
0574

Heather Daveno, Lao Hats, USA
staywarm@laohats.com
www.laohats.com
0670, 0677, 0696, 0697

Paul Davidson, USA
pdavisdon@southplainscollege.edu
0037, 0040–0042

James Matthew Day, Notebook Paper Comics Productions, USA
brayfast@gmail.com
notebookpapercomics.blogspot.com
0208, 0210, 0281, 0335, 0327

Idris De Angeli, Zahira's Boudoir, UK
ldrisdeangeli@zahirasboudoir.com
www.zahirasboudoir.com
0533, 0571, 0573

Kecia Deveney, Lemoncholy's Studio, USA
keeshagirl4@aol.com
www.lemoncholys.blogspot.com
0743, 0744, 0748

Dillon Works!, USA
www.dillonworks.com
0444–0447

Joshua A. Dinunzio, Salty Slug Industries, USA
joe@josephdinunzio.com
www.josephdinunzio.com
0308–0310

Arthur W. Donovan, Donovan Design, USA
www.donovandesign.com
0494–0514

Don Donovan, USA
dondonovan@aol.com
www.flickr.com/photos/23090343@n07/
0876–0883

Laurie Dorrell, Moonwild Art, USA
wildmoon@bassig.com
www.moonwild.blogspot.com
0333

Jazmyn & Logan Douillard, Douillard Custom Creations, Canada
firelightgleam@hotmail.com
bandeau.deviantart.com
0576, 0579

Emperor of the Red Fork Empire, USA
redforkempire@gmail.com
www.redforkempire.com
0113–0116, 0273–0278, 0624, 0625, 0642, 0704, 0705, 0927, 0928

Dominique Falla, Australia
dominiquefalla@me.com
www.dominiquefalla.com
0121–0132

Professor Thaddeus T. Fang a.k.a. artist Anthony J. Rogers III, USA
jollyroger54@hotmail.com
www.professorthaddeustfang.com
0014, 0015

Jessica Faraday, Faraday Bags and Bijoux, USA
jessfaraday@hotmail.com
www.faradaybags.etsy.com
0442, 0443, 0596, 0692, 0693, 0698, 0699

Ian Finch-Feld, Skinz N Hydez, Canada
skinz-n-hydez@live.com
www.skinznhydez.com
0643, 0645–0667

Sarah Fishburn, Designs & Ragtags, USA
sarah@sarahfishburn.com
www.sarahfishburn.com
0235

Kat Fortner-McNiff, USA
blkkatxiii@gmail.com
0627–0630

Eric Freitas, USA
www.ericfreitas.com
0339, 0342, 0344–0348

Christi Friesen, CF Originals, USA
christi@cforiginals.com
www.cforiginals.com
0056, 0057

Kerin Gale, USA
remnants.art@gmail.com
remnantsofolde.com
0839

Penelope Almendros Garcia, Revue Vintage, Spain
www.penelopealmendros.com
0520, 0524, 0525, 0554

Thomas E. Gawron, USA
0176–0178, 0180, 0181, 0638–0641, 0678, 0679, 0890–0894, 0929, 0933–0935

Rainey J. Gibney, The Josie Baggley Company, Ireland
josiebaggley@hotmail.com
www.thejosiebaggleycompany.com
0821

Cole H. Goldstein, Cole Hasting's Modern Antiquities, USA
cole@colehastings.com
www.colehastings.com
0480–0482

Lindsey Goodbun, UK
aldanaart07@gmail.com
www.fantasyfauna.yolasite.com
0258

Jade Gordon, USA
www.jadegordon.com
0214, 0215, 0224

Jonathan Gosling, River Otter Widget Studios, USA
riverotterrustic@aol.com
www.riverotterwidget.etsy.com
0449, 0450, 0911, 0915

Graffiti Technica, Australia
brad@graffititechnica.com
www.graffititechnica.com
0313

Sara Gries, USA
sara013@gmail.com
sara013.etsy.com
0017, 0018, 0038, 0039

Dr. Grymm, Dr. Grymm Laboratories, USA
drgrymm@drgrymmlabortories.net
www.drgrymmlaboratories.net
0001, 0006, 0154–0162, 0231, 0250, 0252, 0253, 0254, 0316, 0326, 0397, 0473, 0608, 0618–0622, 0916, 0939, 0966, 0999, 1000

Kimberly Hart, Monster Kookies, Canada
monster_kookies@hotmail.com
www.monsterkookies.com
0088–0099

Christina "Riv" Hawkes, USA
riv@purpleshiny.com
www.purpleshiny.com
0715, 0717, 0718, 0722, 0848, 0851

Terrill Helander, Art My Way, USA
terrillh@aol.com
www.artmyway.net
0164, 0700, 0701, 0741, 0819

Hilde Heyvaert, House of Secrets Incorporated, Belgium
hildekitten@gmail.com
www.houseofsecretsincorporated.be
0562–0567

Anthony Jon Hicks, Tinplate Studios, USA
tinplatestudios@gmail.com
www.tinplatestudios.etsy.com
0100, 0973–0976

Jen Hilton, USA
jlhjewelry@gmail.com
jlhjewelry.com
0841, 0842

Ned Hobgood, USA
nedhobgood@gmail.com
0232

Peter Hollinghurst, UK
peter@hollinghurst.org.uk
www.hollinghurst.org.uk
0242

Martin Horspool, Australia
info@buggyrobot.com
www.buggyrobot.com
0051, 0133–0146, 0289, 0314, 0337, 0943, 0944

Kristin Hubick, Retro Cafe Art Gallery, USA
krishubick@hotmail.com
www.retrocafeart.com
0723, 0724

Allan K. Hunter, Sirius Werks Phantasmic Phabrications, USA
siriuswerks@gmail.com
0994–0997

InSectus Artifacts, Australia
dr.insectus@gmail.com
www.doctorinsectus.com
0086, 0087, 0773–0776, 0778, 0779

Mike Jennings, USA
mike@hannahgrey.com
0601, 0604

Shoshanah Jennings, Adorning Erzulie, USA
shosh@hannahgrey.com
www.adorningerzulie.com
0754, 0755

Christine Jones, Crimson Chain Leatherworks, USA
leathergeek@hotmail.com
0585

Dan Jones, Tinkerbots, USA
tinkerbots@att.net
0191–0198, 0969–0972, 0986, 0988, 0992, 0993

Sheri Jurnecka, Jurnecka Creations, USA
jurneckacreations@gmail.com
www.jurneckacreations.com
0315, 0317, 0318, 0671, 0863, 0956, 0958

Kammlah.Thayer Collection for Carol Hicks Bolton / E.J. Victor Furniture, USA
sarah@carolhicksbolton.com
www.ejvictor.com
0455, 0458

Erin Keck, E.K. Creations, USA
egk1313@aol.com
www.ekcreations.etsy.com
0428, 0430–0432, 0434, 0845, 0846

Jill Kerns, Altered Ever After, USA
jill@alteredeverafter.com
www.alteredeverafter.com
0726–0733

Louise Kiner, Canada
dksister@aol.com
dksister.daportfolio.com
0236–0239

Joshua W. Kinsey, J.W. Kinsey's Artifice, USA
josh@jwkinseyswoodcraft.com
www.jwkinseysartifice.com
0332, 0336, 0420–0427, 0433, 0435, 0456, 0457, 0468, 0469

Donna Kishbaugh, The Art of Donna, USA
flexoedit@aol.com
www.theartofdonna.wordpress.com
0033

Mel Kolstad, Snizzers & Gwoo, USA
mel@kolstad.net
www.flickr.com/photos/melsatcs
0083–0085

Trisha Krueger, MarySewDesigns, Germany
trisha81@gmail.com
marysew.com
0782–0785, 0847

Rusty Lamer, Scenic Designer; Chip Sullivan, Optic Provocateur, USA
csully4@yahoo.com
rustylamer@gmail.com
www.gonzogardens.com
www.rustylamer.com
0319–0321

Robert LaMonte, USA
guyver_k9@yahoo.com
0021, 0874

Diana Laurence, USA
dianalaurence@wi.rr.com
www.dianalaurence.com
0282, 0285

Cyndi Lavin, USA
cyndi@mazeltovjewelry.com
www.mazeltovjewelry.com
0852, 0859–0862, 0864, 0865

Legion Fantastique, USA
info@legionfantastique.com
www.legionfantastique.com
0519, 0535, 0536, 0572

K.Leistikow, USA
kleistikow@hotmail.com
artofkleistikow.blogspot.com
0225, 0283, 0284, 0912

Jeffrey W. Lilley, USA
generalcaled@gmail.com
generalarmories.deviantart.com
0312, 0392, 0690, 0961, 0963, 0964, 0967

Shawn M. Lopez, USA
shawnmlopez@gmail.com
0753, 0770, 0990

Robert Lucas, Genuine Plastic, USA
rd.lucas@comcast.net
0467, 0945–0955, 0957

Val Lucas, Bowerbox Press, USA
val@bowerbox.com
www.bowerbox.com
0477, 0493

Debbie Lynch, USA
dag17@cox.net
theothersideofdeb.blogspot.com
0837, 0838, 0840

maduncle, Australia
cliffo@three.com.au
www.austeampunk.blogspot.com
0385

Michael J. Marchand and Tim Marchand, Ajar Communications, LLC, USA
mike@ajarcommunications.com
www.ajarcommunications.com
0259–0272, 0597–0599, 0898–0900

Elizabeth Marek, Artisan Cake Company, USA
info@artisancakecompany.com
artisancakecompany.com
0052

Ramon R. Martin, USA
ramonpiper@aim.com
www.etsy.com/shop/ramonpiper
0631, 0632, 0634–0636, 0637

Cassandra Mathieson, Cadaverous Lovely, USA
vintageclassic@gmail.com
www.cadaverouslovely.etsy.com
0605, 0672, 0691

Deryn Mentock, Something Sublime, USA
mocknet@sbcglobal.net
somethingsublime.typepad.com
0735–0740, 0751

Tamara A. Mickelson, T.M. Originals, USA
javagoth@gmail.com
javagoth.etsy.com
0756, 0757, 0759

James Muscarello, USA
muscarelloart@hotmail.com
0287, 0288

Matt Nyberg, Leviathan Steamworks, USA
leviathansteamworks@gmail.com
leviathansteamworks.etsy.com
0758, 0760–0763

Alison Park-Douglas, Velvet Mechanism, USA
alison@velvetmechanism.com
www.velvetmechanism.com
0588, 0589, 0714, 0849, 0850, 0855

Christopher Mark Perez, USA
smilingmonk@gmail.com
www.hevanet.com/cperez
0167–0174

Shirlene Perini, USA
sperini@gmail.com
www.onlyu.etsy.com
0549

Brace Peters, USA
the_braceman@yahoo.com
0484–0486

Patricia Phillips, USA
pttyphllps@lycos.com
0786–0794, 0857

P.J. Pilgrim, Apple Blossom Photography, USA
appleblossomphoto@gmail.com
www.wix.com/appleblossomphoto/appleblossom
0516, 0523, 0526, 0532, 0543, 0552, 0553, 0555, 0584, 0591, 0623

Isaiah Max Plovnick, USA
kosherboy@rcn.com
0150, 0669

Daniel Pon, Paradox Designs, USA
paradox@thetentacleparadox.com
www.thetentacleparadox.com
0459–0462

Regina Portscheller, Omnium-Gatherum Arts, USA
artsy_reg@yahoo.com
http://og-arts.blogspot.com
0229

Daniel Proulx, Catherinette Rings, Canada
daniel.proulx@hotmail.com
catherinetterings.etsy.com
0163, 0165, 0166, 0795–0801, 0810–0818, 0866–0870

Michael Pukáč, USA
michaelpukac@gmail.com
www.michaelpukac.com
0189, 0190, 0199–0203

q phia, USA
qphia1@gmail.com
www.qphia.blogspot.com
0609, 0611, 0616

Captain Jason Redbeard—Royal Gronican Navy, USA
rwhite@wesleyan.edu
http://www.wesleyan.edu/av/gronican.htm
0290–0307

Jenifer J. Renzel, USA
jjrenzel@gmail.com
0179, 0182

Kate Richbourg, USA
katerichbourg@gmail.com
www.beaducation.com
0828

Jeffrey Richter, USA
jeffreyrichter@ymail.com
www.richterfineart.etsy.com
0043–0050

Marina Rios, Fanciful Devices, USA
marmarios@yahoo.com
fancifuldevices.etsy.com
0820, 0822–0826

LF Roberts, Floydagain Designs,
USA
floydagain@gmail.com
www.floydagain.etsy.com
0381–0384

Billie Robson, Art By Canace, USA
canace@hvc.rr.com
www.canace.net
0223, 0233, 0388–0391, 0716, 0769,
0856

Will Rockwell, USA
thisissteampunk@gmail.com
0019, 0029, 0032, 0234, 0429, 0466,
0487

Lisa A. Rooney, USA
crescentmoonschool@gmail.com
www.overthecrescentmoon.blogspot.
com
0448, 0483, 0545–0548, 0550, 0913

Bruce Rosenbaum, Modvic, USA
bruce@modvic.com
www.modvic.com
0472, 0474–0476, 0478, 0479,
0489–0491

Claudia Roulier, USA
claudiaroulier@aol.com
www.claudiaroulier.com
0073

Royal Steamline, USA
allaboard@royalsteamline.com
www.royalsteamline.com
0117–0120

**Lynne Rutter, Lynne Rutter Murals
& Decorative Painting**, USA
lynne@lynnerutter.com
www.lynnerutter.com
0451, 0452

**Barbe Saint John,
Saints & Sinners**, USA
barbe@barbesaintjohn.com
www.barbesaintjohn.com
0222, 0227, 0742, 0806, 0807, 0843,
0844

Michael Salerno, USA
tripletlads@mac.com
0013, 0020, 0395, 0577, 0937

Jane Salley, USA
janesalley@gmail.com
thejaneworld.com
0827, 0829–0832

Larissa Sayer, Canada
cheekyraven@live.ca
ravenriss.blogspot.com
0537, 0968

Markus Schuetz, Germany
markusuetz@gmx.de
0206, 0207, 0209

**Brent Evan Scofield a.k.a.
Professor Quentin Zipcash**, USA
brentnjoan@gmail.com
0764, 0765, 0767, 0871, 0873, 0875

**Amanda Scrivener, Professor
Maelstromme's Steam Laboratory
and Brute Force Studios**, UK
bruteforceleather@bruteforce.com
amanda.scrivener@hotmail.co.uk
profmaelstromme.etsy.com
0771, 0772, 0777

Tom Sepe, USA
thomas@tomsepe.com
tomsepe.com
0923–0925

**Angela Shaffer, Akeishaf's Fusion
Fabrications**, USA
shaffer.angela@gmail.com
www.etsy.com/shop/akeishaf
0752

**Heather Simpson-Bluhm,
Bluhm Studios**, USA
heatherbluhm@yahoo.com
www.bluhmstudios.com
0463, 0464

Martin Small, UK
martin@rubyk.com
www.soulstealer.co.uk
0517, 0518, 0544, 0575, 0600

Deanne Smith, Goldenthrush, USA
sdeannes@aol.com
goldenthrush.deviantart.com
0230, 0578

**Laurel Steven,
Rueschka by Laurel Steven**, USA
laurelsteven@sbcglobal.net
laurelsteven.etsy.com
0750, 0833, 0836

Stefan Stock, Germany
info@stefan-stock.de
www.stefan-stock.de
0917–0922

**Sarah Stocking aka Vespertine
Nova Lark, The Spectra Nova**, USA
spectranova@gmail.com
spectranova.etsy.com
spectranova.blogspot.com
0734, 0834, 0835, 0853, 0854, 0858

**Haruo Suekichi, Suekichi Haruo
Koubou**, Japan
info@tom-c.oo.jp
www.tom-s.co.jp
0606, 0680–0689

Lynda Taft, USA
lynda441@yahoo.com; mpsy28@gmail.
com
themanticoresociety.blogspot.com
0539

**Andrew Tarrant, Trespasser
Ceramics**, Canada
trespasser@trespasser.ca
www.trespasser.ca
0488, 0492

Tim Tate, Washington Glass School,
USA
timtateglass@aol.com
timtateglass.com
0175, 0328, 0329

Janet Teas, USA
janet.teas@gmail.com
0695

**Michael Thee,
Michael Thee Studio, LLC**, USA
michael@michaeltheestudio.com
michaeltheestudio.com
0780, 0781, 0802–0805, 0808, 0809

Erin Tierneigh, USA
whisper@ssicarus.com
www.steampunkworldsfair.com
0540–0542

Topsy Turvy Design, USA
www.topsyturvydesign.com
0515, 0521, 0529–0531, 0560, 0561

**Kendra Tornheim,
Silver Owl Creations**, USA
silverowlcreations@gmail.com
www.silverowlcreations.com
0745–0747, 0749

**Jud Turner, Jud Turner, Sculptor,
LLC**, USA
jud@judturner.com
www.judturner.com
0061–0070, 0074, 0075

Urbandon, Australia
donpezzano@gmail.com
www.urbandon.blogspot.com
0016, 0022, 0025, 0026, 0903–0907,
0909, 0910

Daniel Valdez, USA
smeeon@yahoo.com
www.smeeon.com
0895–0897

Phillip Valdez, USA
phillipvaldez@comcast.net
www.phillipvaldez.com
0204, 0205, 0338

Dr. Tony Valentich, Australia
drtonyvalentich@aol.com
0959, 0960, 0962

**María S. Varela, Model Patricia
Egea, Clothing Penélope
Almendros**, Bavaria
leopardflowers@hotmail.com
0551

Lotus L. Vele, USA
lootsvele@yahoo.com
whymsicallotus.blogspot.com
0255–0257

B. Vermeulen, The Netherlands
endeavourcull@hotmail.com
endeavourcull.etsy.com
0977, 0978

Diana Vick, USA
artvixn@hotmail.com
www.dianavick.com
0279, 0280, 0522, 0527, 0528, 0538,
0558, 0559, 0586, 0587, 0590, 0603,
0987

**The Lord Baron Joseph C.R.
Vourteque IV & Rev. Cpt. Samuel
Flint**, USA
josephcrvourteque@gmail.com
steampunkchicago.com
0009–0012

Jordan Waraksa, USA
sculpture@jordanwaraksa.com
www.jordanwaraksa.com
0008, 0386, 0387, 0884–0889

Danny Warner, USA
dan@designpuck.com
www.designpuck.com
0251, 0322, 0331

Weirdward Work/Arpad Tota,
Hungary
weirdwardworks@gmail.com
www.etsy.com/shop/wwworks
0023, 0024, 0027, 0028, 0030, 0031,
0398–0400

Davin White, USA
davinwhite@gmail.com
steamplatypus.com
0617, 0998

Miriam Wilde, USA
sundogr@comcast.net
0979–0982

Melissa Williams, USA
mdw842003@yahoo.com
www.trancetraveler.blogspot.com
0101–0112, 0335

**Eddie Wilson, whisperstudio
broken toys**, USA
whisperstudio@hotmail.com
etsy.com/shop/whisperstudio
0324, 0325, 0330, 0334, 0633, 0872,
0901, 0902

Roger Wood, klockwerks, Canada
roger@klockwerks.com
www.klockwerks.com
0036, 0147–0149, 0152, 0364–0371,
0401–0414, 0914

**Steve Ziolkowski,
Cinemagician**, USA
spajadigit@gmail.com
0323, 0602, 0936–0938, 0989, 0991

RESOURCES

BRASS GOGGLES BLOG
UK
Steampunk blog
brassgoggles.co.uk/blog

BRASS GOGGLES FORUM
UK
Steampunk forum
brassgoggles.co.uk/forum

BRUTE FORCE STUDIOS
USA
Costume and prop makers
www.bruteforceleather.com

**CHARLES RIVER MUSEUM OF
INDUSTRY & INNOVATION**
USA
History of industry and innovation
www.crmi.org

THE GENTLEMAN'S EMPORIUM
USA
Steampunk clothing supplier
www.gentlemansemporium.com

GILDED AGE RECORDS
USA
Steampunk music record label
www.gildedagerecords.com

THE STEAMPUNK BIZARRE
USA
Annual art exhibit
steampunkbizarre2010.blogspot.com

STEAMPUNK CULTURE
USA
Steampunk videos, links, and art
www.steampunkculture.com

THE STEAMPUNK EMPIRE
USA
Meeting place for Steampunk enthusiasts
www.steampunkempire.com

THE STEAMPUNK HOME
USA
Steampunk furnishings
www.thesteampunkhome.blogspot.com

STEAMPUNK MAGAZINE
UK
Magazine devoted to Steampunk lifestyle
www.steampunkmagazine.com

THE STEAMPUNK TRIBUNE
USA
Global Steampunk resource site
www.steampunktribune.com

THE STEAMPUNK WORLD FAIR
USA
An annual Steampunk event
steampunkworldsfair.com

STEAMPUNKER
Russia
Steampunk resource site
www.steampunker.ru

ACKNOWLEDGMENTS

First and foremost I would like to thank Mary Ann Hall, Tiffany Hill, and the team at Quarry Books for allowing me to work on this wonderful publication with them. I would also like to thank Barbe Saint John for her assistance in pulling this book together.

Very special thanks go out to my wife, business partner, and right side of my brain, Allison DeBlasio, for her constant support and hard work on this project. Without her coordination and organization, this book would not have been possible.

I would be remiss if I did not thank all of the artists who have contributed to this book. It has been an honor to work with all of you on this project. May your creativity continue to build this world of Steampunk that has brought us all together.

Finally, I would like to dedicate this book to my sons and future Steampunks, James and Jack, who give me my inspiration every day.

Sincerely;

Joey Marsocci

a.k.a. Dr. Grymm
Proprietor of Dr. Grymm Laboratories

ABOUT THE AUTHOR

Dr. Grymm's alter ego, Joey Marsocci, along with his business partner and wife Allison DeBlasio, are proprietors of Dr. Grymm Laboratories in Connecticut. Grymm's custom contraptions and sculptures have been seen in Steampunk exhibits, films, television, theater productions, and publications around the world. Most recently, Dr. Grymm, known for his Victrola "Eye-Pod" (a modded iPod) and his Brainstorm Machines, exhibited at the Oxford University History of Science Museum Steampunk Exhibit in 2010, and is also a featured artist at The Cosmopolitan Hotel, opening in Las Vegas in 2011. Annually, Dr. Grymm hosts and curates an international art exhibit, "The Steampunk Bizarre," which is the subject of the documentary *I AM STEAMPUNK* by Neurotic Films.

Visit the official website at: www.drgrymmlaboratories.net

View the online journal at: www.drgrymmlaboratories.com

Learn more about the Steampunk Bizarre Exhibit at: steampunkbizarre2010.blogspot.com